ABOUT THE AUTHOR

Sarmistha Pritam started her career as a contributor to various Assamese newspapers and magazines and is now a well-known name in the contemporary Assamese literary scene. She has won many prestigious awards like the Assam State Government Literary Award (2015), and the Dr. Bhabendra Nath Saikia Memorial Award (2021), among others.

She is also an advocate for people with spinal muscular atrophy, a severe genetic disorder, from which she has been suffering from childhood. Her autobiography, *Atmakathaa*, published in 2011, has since been translated into English and Hindi. Apart from novels, she has also penned a children's book called *Aalfulor Sopun*.

ABOUT THE TRANSLATOR

Ranjita Biswas is an independent journalist, author and award-winning translator. She translates from Assamese and has seven published works to her credit, among which are *Written in Tears* by Arupa Patangia Kalita that won the Best Translation Prize in English from Sahitya Akademi in 2017 and *The Loneliness of Hira Barua*, another of Kalita's books, which won the PFC-Valley of Words Award, 2021.

She has also written a coffee table book, a travelogue and several short stories.

BENEATH THE SIMOLU TREE

Sarmistha Pritam

Translated by Ranjita Biswas

SIMON &
SCHUSTER

London · New York · Sydney · Toronto · New Delhi

First published in India by Simon & Schuster India 2024

Simon & Schuster: Celebrating 100 Years of Publishing in 2024

1 3 5 7 9 10 8 6 4 2

Simon & Schuster India
818, Indraprakash Building,
21, Barakhamba Road,
New Delhi 110001.

www.simonandschuster.co.in

PB ISBN: 978-81-967547-3-0
eBook ISBN: 978-81-967547-1-6

Typeset in India by SÜRYA, New Delhi
Printed and bound in India by Replika Press Pvt. Ltd.

FSC
www.fsc.org
MIX
Paper from responsible sources
FSC® C016779

Simon & Schuster India is committed to sourcing paper that is made from wood grown in sustainable forests and support the Forest Stewardship Council, the leading international forest certification organisation. Our books displaying the FSC logo are printed on FSC certified paper.

1

The sky was resplendent now. Tufts of clouds stained themselves in colour snatched from the gradually setting sun. The scattered clusters, big and small, looked like the strewn remains of a crushed, ripe papaya.

Paridhi was leaning against a bamboo post on the long verandah in front of the house with a sloping roof. Her eyes were fixed on the sky. Despite its magnificence today as it stood on the threshold of evening, she always felt sad at this time of the day. Sure, the sky would be speckled with myriad bright stars soon, but without the sun she felt like an orphan—abandoned. She could not explain this affinity to the sun. When it left for the day, she felt it took away a part of her with it. An intense weariness then overcame her.

She had spent the day painting on pebbles without a break. After a long time, she was able to concentrate on doing something she loved. These days she had to spend a lot of time with her bordeuta, the elder brother of her father. If he did not see Paridhi even for a little while, he called out loudly for her. How much could her mother manage on her own? She was on her toes moving from one room to another, from the kitchen to the bedroom, throughout the day. The old pain in her waist surfaced quite frequently these days. Now there was the additional work of looking after her elder brother-in-law. So Paridhi attended to his demanding call promptly, even if she was busy with other chores.

Paridhi's heart filled with sadness. At one time, she used to hold bordeuta's hand with great faith that she would always be safe with him standing by her side. And now, his hand sought hers. Lately, he had become quite weak and needed assistance to manage even the most ordinary tasks. If he walked a little more than usual, his head would spin and he needed someone by his side to lean on. He even found it difficult to get up from the bed on his own. There was a time when he, Bordeuta, proudly proclaimed that he would never be under anybody's obligation but now, finding himself helpless, he often lost his temper. He ground his teeth in frustration when he could not button up his shirt with his trembling fingers.

Paridhi straightened up. She felt a pain climbing down her neck to her back. It could be because she had been bent over the stones for many hours at a stretch only taking a break only a couple of times to check on her uncle. Today, thankfully, he had not asked for her constantly. He seemed tired, physically and mentally.

The sweet smell of dhuna assailed her nose. She turned

her head to see her mother and said, "Ma, perhaps bordeuta is not very well today. Did he eat properly?"

"Not really. I served him a small amount but even then, he didn't finish it all."

"Did you give him the medicines on time?"

"Yes, I did."

Her mother stepped down to the courtyard with the earthen pot in which the incense was burning. Facing the gate at the entrance of the house, she bowed reverently to the approaching evening. Paridhi's eyes too closed automatically in a prayer. She knew that her god and her mother's god were not the same. Even then, at these moments, somehow their minds converged. A growing sense of foreboding, as if an ancient tree nearby was about to be uprooted, made both of them bow to some unknown force.

Her mother now went into the inner quarters. With a strange sadness that assailed her, Paridhi walked towards her uncle's room. This big house, once full of people, had only three inhabitants now.

"Are you asleep, bordeuta?"

"No. Pari, where were you all this time? I called you so many times."

"I was in the front verandah. That's why I didn't hear you. Why did you call me?"

"Why did I call you? Oh…you see…I've forgotten."

"It's all right. You tell me when you remember," Paridhi replied.

Sitting on the bed, she started giving him a forehead massage. Her uncle asked her if she had locked the doors properly. She assured him that she had. She knew what would follow now. He would warn her that these days things were not the same. People did not feel safe even during the day. Nobody could be trusted. Then he would mumble, "We were much better off in our day" and reminisce. Even with that voice, now weakened by age and illness, he would go on and on, describing many things—his childhood, adolescence, a youth full of many happy tones. He would lose track in between and Paridhi would help him recall.

Her uncle's words were like stories.

Paridhi still loved listening to stories. At one time, her uncle had told her stories of kings and his subjects. The tales about mythical kings and his courtesans would eventually stream into stories of historical figures of royalty and the various court intrigues. Paridhi sometimes felt bored. She would rather listen to stories about the water princess but did not interrupt him.

Her friend, Juroni, knew many stories about the water princess. She would embellish the stories her mother told her the previous evening before narrating them to Paridhi the next day.

Paridhi and Juroni—they were inseparable. Paridhi grew up holding Juroni's hands through her childhood, her adolescence, as they explored the winding lanes of the village, its waterbeds and the jungles around.

When Juroni waved at her, inviting her for one of their exploits, Paridhi felt her legs getting restless and eager to run. Her eyes strayed from the pages of her study books.

It seemed as if these happened just yesterday.

She could see two little girls jumping between the sleepers of the railway track. They waited, sitting on a bench on the platform for a train to pass by. There were many things on which Paridhi and Juroni did not see eye to eye. But on one subject they were absolutely on the same wavelength—both of them wanted to get on a train and go…far, far away. Paridhi did not know the reason behind Juroni's wish. As for herself, there were many.

Sometimes Juroni would get up from the bench and put her ears on the shining track to listen. She would pick up a few stones lying in between the tracks and carry them in her hands before coming to sit again on the bench. She would then try earnestly to make sparks fly by scratching the two stones together. After many attempts, if a spark suddenly flared up she would be overjoyed. Just to see those sparks she would go on and on, despite her many failed attempts.

The approaching red-coloured train with its *g…u…m…g…u…m* sound would make the platform vibrate with impact. Then it would stop just in front of them, the piercing whistle rising up to the sky above. Some passengers would get off, some would get in.

When it left with its row of bogies, like a centipede

with many legs, its pace was slow at first, eventually picking up speed. They had heard that in olden times trains ran on coal. Paridhi imagined a scene often—a sweaty body shovelling chunks of coal into the cavernous firebox of the engine's boiler to make the train gather speed. A few years after their birth, the broad-gauge track was introduced in their area. Now the trains ran quite fast. Till the train left, for whatever reason, Paridhi felt a little disorientated. She felt her head spin a bit too. As she looked at the receding train, and its last compartment with a cross sign painted on its back, she felt a strange kind of grief. She could not fathom why.

How old was she then? Eleven? Twelve?

Perhaps.

As soon as she'd return from school, she would gulp down the rice and curry her mother kept ready and then would scamper over to Juroni's house. Juroni would emerge, wiping her wet palms on her frock. They had the same destination in mind—the railway station.

A concrete road ran through the village dividing it into two. Paridhi and Juroni's houses were next to each other on one side of the road. More than half of the people lived on this side. Fewer people lived on the other side. Across the metal road in front of Juroni's house there was an earthen path that led to the station. There was a big pond by the side of this path. Its water could be used by all. By its side was a krishnachura tree. Its branches drooped down to the pond. In the month of Fagun, heralding spring, the tree painted pictures on the water below in blood red. The pond's water too seemed eager to borrow some colour from the flaming red sky above, to dress itself in crimson glory.

Did people also hanker for colours like this—with such keen yearning? Paridhi's adolescent mind often wondered.

On the elevation near the bank of the pond, there were many wild garlic plants. Paridhi almost habitually pick up a few of their white flowers when she passed by. At the end of the earthen path there was a hog plum tree. If you took a left turn from there, the station came into view.

The station was quite tiny. Only a few houses with red tin roofs and white walls. At a little distance in front of these houses were three jackfruit trees. A stone bench rested underneath. The waiting room was a short distance away. By the side of the forecourt there were three stone benches. If you sat in the middle one and turned your back to the track you could make out the vague silhouettes of their village surrounded by trees, looking almost like a water colour painting.

Next to the waiting room was the ticket counter. Its tin roof was painted a dark green. Attached to the small verandah in front of the ticket counter stood a pole from which hung a bell. As the train approached, the assistant to the station master came out with a foot-long rod and rang the bell.

A little away from the ticket counter was another bench, not of stone but of wood. Three long pieces of wood were put side by side to form the seat and three others horizontally for them to lean on. Sitting here, Paridhi spent time either chatting with someone or silently absorbing the beauty of nature. From here, she would often stare at the sun. This is when she often thought of hopping into one of the compartments of the train and going away somewhere.

Though she went around the lanes and by-lanes of the village with Juroni absorbing the beauty of the myriad colours around them, Paridhi's childhood and adolescence were buried in the darkness of fear and uncertainty. Uncertainty due to her deuta, her father.

Deuta. Deuta. Paridhi ran her tongue over the word silently.

For most people in this world, the word perhaps symbolised the welcome shade of a banyan tree or a strong hand on one's head assuring that no evil power could harm his dear child. For Paridhi, the word meant something entirely different. Of shaking in fear at night; a sudden shadow blackening a sunny day; a strange discovery of what a man could be.

He was a strange man.

"Why is he so angry all the time?"

When she questioned her mother thus, the answer ricocheted from her mother's helpless eyes. The angry sparks in his eyes that did not need much provocation to flare up frightened her. She ran away and hid, crawling into the safety of the space underneath a cot in the bedroom. The damp darkness under the bed wrapped the little girl with reassuring hands.

The man got furious even at small things. If the curry had a little less salt, or more, he threw the bell-metal plate to the floor. Paridhi's mother did not have the power to calm her raging husband. She tried to digest his ugly, abusive words silently while picking up the rice grains from the floor. Paridhi got used to seeing such scenes time and again. She witnessed how her mother's hands got dirty while trying to clean the floor where rice grains, curry and water made an unholy mix. Standing at the door of the kitchen, her little heart felt the pain of her mother's suffering. Ah! Those were the very same hands that fed her lovingly a mix of rice and fish curry, rubbed Boroline on her cheeks before putting her to sleep, and ran them over her head softly at night...

"How awful, Ma! Your hand has mud all over."

"My dear, it will be clean as soon as I wash it. Please go from here. Otherwise you will slip on the wet floor."

Of course, the mud could be washed away. But what about the layers of dirt that silted in her mother's mind? Could she wash them away? Paridhi was too young at that time to go deeply into these questions. But once she grew up, she felt depressed thinking about it. She slipped one too many times on the floor of the kitchen—wet and dirty with water and wasted food, thanks to her father's violent temper—to forgive him.

As a child, Paridhi often lost her balance trying to hold onto something solid. She was not alone. Her adolescent elder brother's legs trembled too. Was that why he was getting defiant—like someone whose tongue was so used to curries cooked with too many chillies—that now it didn't even recognise their heat?

Paras, her brother, was about four years older to her. Paridhi never addressed him with the suffix 'dada' as befits an elder brother. She just called him Paras. He was not interested in studies but loved cinema. When he was supposed to learn by rote theories of geometry, he mimicked dialogues of heroes and villains. When he was in the eighth standard, he failed his exams. His back bore the signature of their father's cane whip. By then Paridhi was old enough to feel the pain behind the tears her brother refused to shed.

"Pari! Go, call your brother for lunch," her mother instructed her.

"Will he eat today, Ma?"

"Why not? What's wrong with the food? He won't sit at the study table, the whole day, he will roam around or watch TV. And now that he has failed to get a promotion, what shall his father do other than beat him? Should he kiss his son lovingly? He's been punished rightly. Go, call him!"

Paridhi could feel the rough edge on her mother's voice. She withdrew from the kitchen, her head bowed. Her mother was still mumbling angrily. From the next room she heard her father's loud snoring. Paridhi was outraged that the man who beat up his son so severely was now snoring after having a full meal. She walked fast towards the station. She knew instinctively that Paras was sitting there. Like Paridhi, he went to the station platform when he felt dejected.

Perhaps sorrowful people usually went to the station because they wanted to go away somewhere.

Paridhi emerged from her childhood memories and came back to the present.

These days her bordeuta also talked constantly about going away somewhere.

Paridhi and her uncle sat next to one another, each lost in their own worlds of memories. Her uncle talked constantly as she massaged his forehead. After a while he stopped. He was tired.

He breathed faster and opened his mouth to suck in more air. Slowly his eyes closed. Paridhi kept looking at him.

Again, she wondered at the great change in that familiar figure. His eyes were now sunken. His once protruding midriff, like a pot, had now shrunk so much that it almost touched his spine. His dried-up hands and feet were a portrait of blue and green veins. The underarms were like two holes where one could sink a fist. His once muscled, strong body was now devoid of flesh.

Where did the flesh disappear to, Paridhi often wondered. Time; yes, time had drained the man's body.

Time drained out everybody. Time turned bodies full of life and vigour into faded, monochromatic entities.

Time is so difficult to understand. Sometimes it is kind, sometimes cruel.

Still lost in thought, Paridhi absent-mindedly put up the mosquito net and tucked the ends into the mattress before leaving the room. She did not forget to switch off the light when she went out. Her uncle preferred to be surrounded by darkness these days.

2

The thirst of a man's soul, how intense it is!

When she saw the stones, she felt as if she were a person in famine-struck Somalia now being offered a plate of food.

"Ah, how beautiful!" she uttered the words spontaneously as Mayur took out the stones from his cotton bag and spread them on the floor.

"Where did you get them?"

Mayur was silent for some time.

"Now, tell me!" Paridhi nagged him.

"From here!" Mayur pointed to his chest.

"What do you mean?"

"Well, you yourself tell me nowadays that my heart has become like a slab of stone. So I have taken out a few from there."

"Well, if your chest is now full of such rounded, smooth stones, it's not a bad thing. I can put life into them," Paridhi laughed.

"Yes, you can. Why not? You are like the jiwandhari gem that can bring life to static objects."

Mayur's tone was not teasing; he said it with utmost sincerity.

"Aren't you being too effusive?" Paridhi replied softly.

Though she teased Mayur outwardly, at heart she was rather pleased with the comparison to the holy gem. But was she worth the praise? She did not know what this thirst was that drove her to set off on a journey to pour out her inner feelings—whether on the grey stones or blank pages of an exercise book, trying to transform them into something else. Of course, she knew well enough that she was not an expert in either.

As he saw Paridhi running her fingers on a small smooth stone the colour of a bamboo shoot, Mayur sighed audibly and commented, "Ah, had I been that stone...!"

Paridhi heard him all right but pretended not to. She shifted her eyes from Mayur and tightened her fingers around the stone. Then she almost ignored him and got busy examining the rest of the pile.

Paridhi could not remember when this love for pebbles grew in her. Whenever she saw pretty round stones, she picked them up and after a thorough cleaning, preserved them as if they were made of gold. She filled a huge glass jar with the stones and from time to time she spread them out on the floor to inspect them. Somehow she felt they demanded something from her. She enjoyed looking at each as it lay ensconced in her palm, pretty and unique in shape. One day she saw a man's face on a flat, round stone. She did not have the talent of a great sculptor who spent days shaping a figure but she painted on it in the likeness of a man's face—his nose, his eyes, his lips. And her thirst for more grew. From then on started an acute desire to transform the stones into something else, endowing them with a life of their own with her paintbrush.

Paridhi sat near the bamboo basket filled with stones that lay silent as if asleep. One by one she picked them up and ran her fingers fondly over them. She did it for no other reason than for the sheer pleasure of it.

Long ago she had read somewhere that the practice of painting on stones goes back thousands of years. In 1889, in a place called Mas d'Azil in southwestern France, archaeologists discovered almost fourteen hundred painted stones in a cave. They were painted in ochre, in circular lines, dots, and dashes which perhaps indicated some words or numbers.

Oh, she had forgotten to thank Mayur for the pebbles. He had gone to a lot of trouble to collect them. The thought made her guilty. But was it necessary to thank him verbally? In her heart she was ever so grateful to him. To her, they were not just stones, they were like a plate of rice in the time of famine; a voice articulating the voiceless.

She had, by now, painted almost a hundred stones. But her thirst for painting could not be quenched—on the contrary, it only increased. Where would she find her desired pebbles? In the riverbed? In the hills? She needed stones that were smoothened and polished by water over time. Somebody had told her that one could find beautiful stones around the town of Tezpur on the north bank of the Brahmaputra. Should she tell Bondeep, her beau, 'Let's go on a trip to Tezpur'? But she decided against it. Her pride pulled her back. She wanted to go on her own, something that had yet not happened. But she was getting increasingly restless at the shortage of pebbles in her kitty. Again and again, she felt that when you dammed up some desires, the pain only increased.

Perhaps Mayur understood her inner need. He did not dismiss her thoughts as a luxurious sentiment. So he had gone to Bhalukpung on the Arunachal Pradesh border near Tezpur even if it meant taking off from work and now had surprised her with a sack of carefully selected stones in many shapes. Paridhi's mind filled with softness for Mayur. Something she expected Bondeep to do, or wanted him to understand even though she did not utter the need in so many words, Mayur did instead. He understood.

"What do I say to you, Mayur? What kind of relationship binds me to you?" Paridhi mused, her eyes closed.

She took a deep breath and then started selecting the stones from among the pile. Some were small like grapes, some oval, some big enough to size up to one third of a foot. And look, in so many hues! In shades of wheat, black, golden Muga, red and some sparkled like the skin of Chanda fish. Which ones should she select for her painting? They all seemed to beg her, please choose me, please colour me. Paridhi looked at them again with concentration.

What kind of wish did each have? Which one of them desired a particular colour?

She only painted on them, but each came to her with its own personality, its own introduction embedded within.

Stones. Beautiful children of nature.

She spent the whole morning with them. She spread some painted ones on a tray to dry and selected about ten from the rest. To her, some looked like faces of women, she just had to paint the eyebrows, hair and lips to transform them. Her brush would now alter some stones into owls, some to fish and others to sleeping cats. The toe-sized ones would be painted in red or green and with dots in black they would look like ladybirds. Looking at the oval black stone in her palm, Paridhi wondered aloud, "And what do you want for yourself?"

Its cold touch intrigued her.

A mermaid, maybe? "Mermaid," Paridhi pronounced the word silently a few times.

Her dreamy childhood stories twirled around the mermaid. When she remembered the story Juroni's mother told her about the young daughter of the ocean king, sadness clouded her mind. A prince fell in love with a princess swimming in the sea. He, however, had not seen her beautiful face. He did not even know that she was a mermaid. Her lower portion, like a fish's tail, was immersed in water. The prince only saw her long, shining hair and heard the sweet song she sang. He carried in his heart the echo of that lovely song to the palace and found himself thinking about her all the time. Soon rumours floated in the air about his love for the princess of the water and his desire to marry her. But he did not know her real identity and that without water, she would die. To marry her beloved prince the mermaid approached the magician. The wily man wanted her sweet voice in exchange of turning her tail into two human legs. She was ready to discard her long fish-tail for the prince and was even ready to lose her voice.

For love, maybe one can sacrifice even the most cherished asset. So the princess who loved to sing, chose silence. But the poor girl did not know that for the prince, her sweet voice was the only thing that attracted him to her. Without her singing voice he did not recognise her at all. So she had to return to the water but was lost forever; without her fishtail she could not swim.

She remembered vaguely reading a story, perhaps a story from a foreign land, similar to the one Juroni's mother had told them. Was it written by Hans Christian Andersen? But how did the illiterate woman know a story from a far-off land, Paridhi often wondered, as also at the reach of stories that can travel across lands and oceans through time.

Looking at the cold stone, she wondered how a mermaid, though swimming in water, could still be thirsty.

A sigh escaped Paridhi. She herself had seen many who were still thirsty even though living in the midst of water. The twenty-five-year-old girl found herself caught in many of life's riddles. Outwardly, she presented a vivacious front but her inner self was often shadowed by melancholy.

Why was there so much thirst for something in us humans?

Why were people so unhappy? And restless?

The questions often troubled her. Trying to find answers, her thoughts travelled through the veins to her soul—like roots of a tree on wet earth—and then she felt like writing something. In her own small village, there were so many real stories, lives that could be grist for novels. Her own life was intermingled with these life-stories. She could not imagine herself apart from them.

To be truthful, she was not that interested in writing. She did not dream of becoming a successful writer. She wrote out of compulsion. The stories that ensconced themselves in her conscious and subconscious mind nudged her urgently from time to time and then she could not ignore them.

Sometimes, Paridhi thought idly, perhaps people all over the world have the same sensibilities deep down, only the environment or the things surrounding them are different. So when one is sure that the thoughts and ideas that run through the mind in private suddenly find resonance in somebody else's sensibilities, there is surprise, delight even.

Paridhi felt the same way many times. As in the case of Parijat, Nepal's famous writer:

To create literature is not my
interest
but my compulsion.

When time
disturbs
my peace, only then does my pen
move

How uncannily they matched Paridhi's feelings. Like Parijat, Paridhi too was compelled to pen the words. She felt an urgent need to narrate stories that made her restless. Like the stones she painted responding to their invitation to give them character and colour.

The more the stories chased her, the more her pen gathered pace. Sometimes she paused in self-doubt. Would readers be interested in these so-called ordinary characters, and such untold stories lying asleep somewhere? What was the use of knowing about these people? At one time, she waited impatiently to listen to the story of the water princess from Juroni's mother. Did anyone wait for her stories the same way?

Though some of those images turned opaque, others appeared suddenly, like a ray of sunlight penetrating through the winter mist. Every Sunday morning, she used to go to Tilok uncle's house in the village holding on to her bordeuta's finger to watch episodes of *Mahabharata* on the TV. She was too young to understand everything but she recognised the characters because her uncle had told her the stories from the epics. They had to walk almost a kilometer to reach Tilok uncle's house. Did her little legs ache under the strain? No, no, she was too excited at the prospect of watching the figures from her fantasy world coming alive on the screen to worry about pain. She and her uncle were not the only ones. It seemed that half the village turned up—the young, the old, little children, you name it—to watch the *Mahabharata* episodes. With two bars on the sides, the TV set looked like a box. The shutter was a part of the set too. The room was quite big but rather bare of furniture, perhaps kept like that in consideration of the huge audience. People sat wherever they found space, most of them sitting cross-legged on the floor.

Everybody was interested in the stories from the *Ramayana* and the *Mahabharata*. Paridhi's uncle often said, "Without them our childhood is colourless, our youth pale and unexciting, and a consolation not even in cursed old age."

All this happened not so long ago. But everything changed very fast. Like her favourite yellow frock with polka dots, which one day she suddenly found was too short for her. These days nobody has to go to somebody else's house to watch a TV programme. Now the stories reach them effortlessly. The coloured screen features many 'hot' stories, characters enter people's private domain from beyond geographical borders. Maybe people get so drawn into these stories from beyond that they do not bother to know the stories about the people around them. So why should they wait to listen to stories of an ordinary girl like Paridhi? Who would be interested in discovering stories behind the hard stones when so many other attractive things existed?

Paridhi looked again at the oval stone in her palm. Ah, would the youngest daughter of the ocean king emerge from its womb? Like a man urgently seeking something in the warm, soft breasts of a woman, she touched the cold stone and tried to imagine the cool body of the water princess.

3

Paridhi was struck by another thought. Was she neglecting her writing by paying all her attention to the stones?

She had started writing a story a few days ago. As she painted on the pebbles, she did not want to think about it; it irritated her. She had not picked up the pen for some days now. The story of the elderly lady who ran to the railway station as soon as she heard the whistle was stuck somewhere in the writing pad.

It was true, she admitted to herself. The fingers that curled around the paint brush were reluctant to go back to holding the pen. It often happened like this for her. When the words tumbled down from the pen, her mind hesitated to go back to colour palette, and when she was busy mixing colours in the earthen plate till her thirst to create the images were satisfied, she did not feel like writing. So she was a slave to both, her allegiance divided between painting and writing. Sometimes she felt as if she were on a boat in the middle of a river, dithering between the two banks. Which one was the right one to head for?

For the last few days, her daily task of typing pages of a book had also suffered and was paused midway. Bondeep must be upset with her, she thought. He had given her a non-fiction manuscript of about three hundred pages almost a month ago. She had not completed it yet, busy with this or that. Like other tasks, this too Paridhi did with utmost sincerity. She saw to it that there were no typos. This was why Bondeep trusted her with most of the work of his publishing house. But sometimes she got bored. Her eyes were taxed to the limit. These days she had to use glasses while working. But she was compelled to do it for her own sake too. This meant she could be self-reliant and could meet her personal expenses even if they were not luxuries. Her love of writing and painting also helped her in some way. She did them because of her own inner compulsion. She was not interested in appearing for tests one after another in order to obtain a government job. The word 'test' had always put her off, in the past, and even now. Yet, life tested her relentlessly.

Jebhabei tumi shokal dekho, surya is the same.

(Whichever way you look at the morning, the sun is the same.)

The phone came alive with the ringtone in singer Suvomita's sweet voice.

Mayur!

"How are you, stone-princess? How far are you with your painting?"

"Trying to finish in between other work."

"Now tell me how many you have painted so far?"

"About two hundred."

"Can you manage to do about five hundred? Enough for a solo exhibition?"

"Let me see when I can reach the target. Where are you now?"

"At Manas Sanctuary."

Paridhi was not surprised. The boy in love with butterflies was himself like one, flitting from here to there restlessly. He said he would die if he could not wander amidst the jungles. He was someone most comfortable in a sylvan landscape; how could he become dry like a stone? If he called her after the gap of a few days, she teased him, "Your heart has turned into a stone, I think. You haven't even enquired if I am alive or dead."

"What do I do? The jungle has enticed me," he would reply.

Mayur had been researching the butterflies of Assam for the past few months. Sometimes he sent images of the beautiful insects to her through WhatsApp.

"I've just sent a picture of Manas. Check."

Mayur disconnected the line abruptly.

Paridhi checked her phone. A carpet of stones in a variety of colours—black, red, muga, white, blue tinted. In the distance, a row of blue hills and above them, a canopy of white clouds.

"It'll be so lovely to watch the hills sitting on these rocks," Paridhi replied.

Mayur was still online. He replied, "Yes, it's very lovely. Come here one day. We'll spend the whole day watching the hills, sitting on the rocks. Only you and I. We will forget about everything."

"Sure, one day," Paridhi wrote and switched off WhatsApp messenger.

Why did she snub Mayur subtly when she very well knew he meant well? She was not sure what actually played in Mayur's mind, but sometimes in between their conversations he said something casually that stopped her midway. Did he expect something more from her? Maybe he did not really mean anything and just uttered the words carelessly? He was well aware of her relationship with Bondeep. Could she go away for a day to enjoy the beauty of the hills in Mayur's company? Even if there was no ulterior motive in Mayur's invitation, she could not respond to him instantly. She knew if she told Bondeep about the intended outing, he would not say anything but in private he would fume. Could she herself remain unaffected if she came to know that Bondeep had gone away with Ananya for a day to enjoy nature's beauty?

No, the whole thing about relationships was quite complicated and troublesome.

She did not have the energy to analyse all these emotions now. She put aside her restiveness and concentrated on her work. The supple body of the mermaid was taking shape on the oval stone's surface. The ends of the fishtail veering to the left now kissed the muga-coloured locks cascading down from the top of the pebble. The hair on her right, like the twisted tail of a snake, covered her naked breasts. To make the scales of the orange-coloured fishtail look more real, Paridhi chose a thin brush and painted semi-rounds in white on them.

Who was this woman?

The girl who got lost at sea or the one who made Nabakumar, a boy from the village, fall madly in love with her?

Where did the lovely princess disappear to?

Was she imprisoned deep down under the pond by the evil spirit of Jolshai dangoria who lived in the big pond?

Paridhi felt as if all the things around her—the colours, paintbrushes, pebbles, pail of water, the pieces of cotton cloth used to wipe the brushes—were disappearing from view one by one. The wall near her melted away and in its place she found an ever-expanding, bare field.

She remembered the zig-zag, narrow path that ran from her house through the bamboo grove and ended in a field. Almost in the middle of the field where the path veered, there was a huge banyan tree. It was not just a tree but a sentinel protecting the field. At a little distance, sitting on a narrow lane there, she could see Juroni's mother. Her green-bordered sador was carelessly thrown on her left arm. On both sides sat Juroni and Paridhi. Jayanti khuri, Jayanti-aunty, as she called Juroni's mother, came here at midday with her pet goats to graze. Till they finished, the girls did not want to let go of this opportunity. Their incessant begging eventually made the woman relent. When Juroni and Paridhi saw her wetting her tongue, sitting up a little straighter while pulling up her *oroni* on her head, they knew they had won. She would now tell them a story of their choice.

"Can you see that banyan tree? Once upon a time there was a pond near it. A huge tank, actually. The water in that tank was always full to the brim, even in the bone-dry summer months. A young man from the village, Nabakumar, went fishing there every day. He was so fond of angling, that immediately after lunch he made a beeline to its bank and stayed on till late into the afternoon."

Juroni's mother was illiterate, but she told the stories very beautifully, describing every detail.

When Nabakumar came home, his body smelled of raw fish. The wind carried that smell and people knew Nabakumar was returning home. But they were surprised that his khaloi, his cane basket, had only a few fish despite him spending hours by the tank. Sometimes not even that, he returned home with an empty khaloi. But he did not seem disappointed at all. The khaloi of his mind was full; someone had filled it with silver and golden fish.

"Who?" the girls would ask, their eyes rounded in anticipation.

"The Water Princess."

Nabakumar was enticed by the Water Princess. As soon as he arrived with the fishing rod and then dipped it in with the bait, the Water Princess emerged from under the water rowing her golden boat. Was she like this image on the pebble, her full breasts bare, who mesmerised the young man called Nabakumar? Paridhi added a bit of fantasy to the tale from her childhood.

She smiled to herself. She finished painting the fish-tail and then put two white spots for the irises of the eyes. Now she sat still and looked minutely at the recently painted pebble.

Where did the Water Princess get lost?

Did she end up as a Stone Princess at the bottom of the big pond?

Snapping out of her reverie, Paridhi could now feel her neck ache. She closed her eyes and sat with her face upturned for some time. If her mother saw her now she would definitely get a scolding. She lost her temper when she saw her daughter hunkered over the pebbles for hours. At night, she found Paridhi tossing from side to side, troubled by pain and burning eyes. But did her mother know that the mind, forever thirsty to create something, didn't care about physical pain?

What's today's date? How many days of the month of Fagun were gone?

She checked the calendar on her mobile phone. Oh no, it was 24th February, already ten days of Fagun gone. She had only three to four days to submit the story. Paridhi wrote only when she felt like and these few days were not enough, at least for her. Why didn't she say no?

"Paridhi, you must write a story for the Bihu special magazine this time."

Nabaneeta baideu's voice as the assistant editor of the *Anneswan* magazine did not sound like a request but a command. Paridhi had said then, 'I'll try,' to avoid a commitment.

"I won't listen to 'I'll try'. You'll have to. Please send it by the 27th. I'll send the mail ID by SMS. Bye!"

What was this attraction to the railway station?

Was it because the long whistle as it approached the platform carried with it a message about an unknown land beyond... or was it something else?

Whatever it was, when Paridhi sat on the bench at the platform she found a kind of peace. The sense of security she craved for, but never found at home, was here in this open area.

Beyond the railway track on the other side was a huge open field. The villagers by turn cultivated different varieties of paddy there—Ahu, Sali, Aijong. Even sugarcane and mustard grew very well. Behind the village there was another open field but there people cultivated only rice. In winter, when the yellow mustard flowers covered the field, Paridhi, Juroni and many other children from the village skipped around amidst them like butterflies. Suddenly, one of them would shout, "Look, look, there goes Pari's father!"

When she saw the man walking with unsteady steps

near the railway track the girl flying like a butterfly suddenly felt as if she was pierced by thorns of a prickly Siju plant. Her delicate wings fell off. Fearing that her father would see her, Paridhi would kneel down on the ground immediately to hide behind the screen of yellow flowers. She knew that her father would approach the stationmaster to borrow some money.

Ever since she could remember, Paridhi had never seen her father doing anything substantial. All he did was borrow money from people and spend it on alcohol. Afterwards, he made sure to show off his power as a husband to her poor mother. In the name of keeping a watch over his wards' welfare and establishing his right as a father, he put fetters on Paras and Paridhi's ankles. The man who lost his temper if the curry had just a little less salt—did he ever bother to find how the cost of mustard oil and salt was met? Thank God Paridhi's bordeuta worked as a teacher in the village highschool; otherwise they would have had to literally tie their bellies with gamosas to deaden the hunger pangs. Her khura, her father's younger brother, worked in Guwahati and had settled down there with his family. He visited the village only on special occasions like Bihu or some other festival. Later, even those visits trickled down. In his youth her uncle used to play the khol, the hand-held drum. It was now hanging in a corner of their verandah at the back of the house covered in dust and cobwebs

Even when Paridhi was quite young, her father had decided to have a separate kitchen from his elder brother's.

The house was divided into two parts, but the courtyard remained common between the two houses. Paridhi's mother was on tenterhooks, worrying if even the courtyard would be segregated with a bamboo fence. She wept silently for quite a while following the day when everything was divided between the brothers—the land, the kitchen utensils, everything.

For Paridhi, these were too distant events to remember very well. But while growing up, she had witnessed many quarrels between brothers in the village. She remembered well the one between Jon-dada's father and his younger brother.

The brothers were Brahmins. Jon-dada's father was a priest and his uncle practiced as a homeopath doctor. Their houses were separate but near enough to hear anyone even clearing their throat. Nobody in the village knew how the first sparks flew between the two brothers, but suddenly they witnessed a quarrel drumming up. They surmised that it was a regular quarrel between brothers involving land or property. Anyway, if one of them came out to the verandah to shout loudly, the other responded from his side of the fence equally loudly. Their voices would rise steadily, soon reaching a crescendo. Then the cantankerous duo would descend to their respective courtyards and shout at each other standing face to face across the bamboo fence. The yelling subsided slowly; both seemed to get tired after some time, their tempers seemed to simmer down too. One of them perhaps felt his blood pressure shoot up suddenly. "Please calm down, calm down please," was all that the wives of both the brothers could meekly and repeatedly request, feeling helpless. But who would listen to them? Then one wife would drag a chair and the other a cane murha, a stool, to the courtyard for their respective husbands to sit down. Even then, both men would challenge each other with blood-shot eyes. The wives could now be seen fanning their husbands with cane bisonis, hand fans, in an attempt to cool their heads.

But why did other people have to leave their tasks half-done to enjoy these theatrics? Paridhi was puzzled at times. After a few days, when the same pair of brothers was seen sitting next to each other on the bamboo bench in front of their houses and chatting amicably, the onlookers lost interest.

People liked to watch others fight, Paridhi concluded.

Why do people fight so much? What do they want?

She could not find answers.

Paridhi's bordeuta often cited words from the Gita while discussing something. In the afternoon, while sitting on the front verandah as his eyes rested on the sky, now coloured like reddish Jetuka leaves, he often uttered, as if in a soliloquy, "What things did you bring with you, what things will you take back? What is yours today will be someone else's tomorrow, remember."

He was someone who did not crave for land or trifles; he did not want to divide everything into segments for ownership. He wanted to live in harmony with others in the family. But he had to bow down to his brother, Paridhi's father's constant harassment. Her Bborma, his wife, frankly was not that averse to the idea of separate kitchens. Her husband was the only earning member in the family. How many people could be maintained on a school teacher's salary? She had to think about her own children's future too. But even when the kitchens were separated, her uncle bought groceries necessary for two households. Paridhi's mother accepted these with hesitation. In her mind she could see the unhappy face of her elder sister-in-law. That was why she often cooked curries with dhekia, fiddlehead fern, or yams collected from the open field. Behind the courtyard she made her son fashion a bamboo scaffolding with his inexperienced hands. On it climbed creepers of bottle gourd and ribbed gourd. She cooked curries with these vegetables.

The house had been built by Paridhi's grandfather. On the front wall, constructed with earth mixed with a bit of cement and crisscrossed with wooden battens, there was a swastika sign drawn with vermillion. Her mother told Paridhi that it was an auspicious sign. It was almost invisible now as the wall got whitewashed with lime from time to time. Paridhi often ran her fingers over it, believing it to be a sign of progress.

But did Paridhi manage to go forward and walk ahead despite her father scattering sharp stones on her path? Could the fire-spitting father obliterate the dreams ensconced in her growing young body? Perhaps not. And as to her brother Paras, he did not stop watching films either. After school, when he watched films on the TV in somebody else's house, his father went searching for him. But when he returned home he found his son at the study table apparently busy with his books. Paras entered the house through the backyard door after running through the bamboo grove. Paridhi cringed in fear, worrying her father would find out. Now relieved, she complained nonetheless, "You are going to get it one of these days, I tell you. Have you ever thought what will happen if you are found out?"

"Oh, it hasn't happened, right? Forget about all these 'would haves'," Paras would reply airily.

"Please don't do it again. You may not always be lucky."

"*Don ko pakarna muskil hi nahi, namumkin hai.*"

As he pulled up the collar of his shirt and mimicked the dialogue of a famous hero, Paridhi could not help bursting out in laughter despite still being scared.

Paras, however, was quite nervous when his cousin, Rupak, second son of their bordeuta, came home. He was studying in Cotton College in Guwahati. On his visits home he checked Paras' progress in studies. At these times, Paras was not the daring Don but a trembling wet cat.

That year, Paras was in class ten. One day she found a letter between the pages of his book. In one breath, a little fearful, she read the letter. Paras had addressed it to Kabita, his classmate. Though she was quite young—she was in class six then—Paridhi had a vague idea that her brother's letter was not just a collection of words, but he was painting a rainbow for Kabita. She folded the letter carefully the same way and kept it back where she had found it. After that, whenever she saw her brother, the image of a pretty girl wearing mekhela-sador neatly on her way to school floated into her mind. She did not know if the rainbow also coloured Kabita's sky. She meant to ask, but it never happened.

Paridhi was growing up too. She was at an age when someone could appear in her dreams. Did she feel the same way for anyone? Did she want someone to paint a rainbow of words for her, like her brother did for Kabita, and send it across to her in a paper roll? No, it didn't happen. Paridhi was too fearful. As soon as a prince riding a white horse wanted to take up space in her mind, another image took over. That of her mother, whose arms and back bore dark signatures—like ink on paper—thanks to her father. She often wondered if in the intimacy of the night her father ever ran his fingers tenderly on those marks. She would never know.

On some nights, when she woke up and did not find her mother next to her in bed, Paridhi lay curled up like their dog sleeping on the verandah. Automatically her mind sought out some unknown force. She wanted to get up and write something on the pages of her exercise book. In fact, she did write:

Please sing me a lullaby
And, shut the door of grief

Or, take me away from here
Somewhere far away
Open the path to your womb again, Ma
Keep me hidden in your womb, in its darkness, Ma
There's no other place safer than here
Nowhere else

Each page of the diary that Paridhi maintained meticulously, ended with these lines.

4

"Pari... Hei Pari... come here please, can you hear me, dear?"

"Coming, bordeuta!" Paridhi called out. She was getting ready to go for her shower but now slipped on a pair of sandals and went towards her uncle's room. If he called, she had to go straight away, otherwise he would lose his temper. Though she and her mother both tried their utmost to cater to his every need, he complained a lot these days, nonetheless. Even Paridhi, who once was his favourite child in the house, did not escape his grumblings. She could not remember exactly when this new behaviour had started. She always respected and loved her elderly uncle and had never seen him angry like this. His nature was the opposite to her father's.

"Do you want anything, bor-ta?" Paridhi asked in a loud voice. His auditory sense had also deteriorated.

"Do something," he told her and asked her to fetch from the wooden almirah the leather bag where he kept his important documents and cash. She did as instructed, but then he asked her to put it back. He often did this kind of thing these days. Paridhi understood why—he wanted to be reassured that things were in place. He was apprehensive all the time that someone would take them on the sly. In fact, sometimes he even made Paridhi open the almirah at midnight. Woken up at that unearthly hour, Paridhi would get irritated at his unreasonableness but then she controlled herself. Her uncle was like a child now, what was the point of losing her temper? Even though she and her mother hovered around him, looking after him to the best of their ability, he behaved like a lonely, insecure child.

Who is secure and safe in this world anyway, Paridhi thought often. Someone was here yesterday but not anymore today. Who gets lost, who dies in their sleep, nobody can predict these things. The poem in her diary written in her adolescence sometimes stirred and woke her up and she felt like reciting it silently:

Open the path to your womb again, Ma
Keep me hidden in your womb, in its darkness, Ma
There's no other place safer than here
Nowhere else

Once someone enters the world from their mother's womb as a newborn baby, do they ever find such a safe and secure corner? All through life the search continues.

Now before her uncle could ask for anything else, she hurried to the bathroom to have her shower. She had a lot of tasks lined up for the day. First, she had to be off to the bank to withdraw her uncle's pension money, then to pay the electricity bill, then to the store to purchase groceries for the month, then to the pharmacy to buy her mother's high-pressure tablets, and also to the post office to post some important documents. Paridhi tried to recall if she had left anything else missing from the list.

If Paras were here she wouldn't have had to worry about everything like this. As she thought about her brother, the old pain shot up. His innocent face, and the way he treated her, like a friend, stoked her memory. Her ears filled with his hero-like dialogue delivery—

"*Zindagi na milegi dubara*. We don't get a second life. So we should enjoy all the things in this life. We should be like the wind. Don't be afraid to live like the wind. Remember, *jo dar goya woh mor goya*."

The pain in her chest was almost unbearable now. How could she ignore it? Tears flowed down her cheeks incessantly.

The bathroom is the best place to shed tears.

"Before you go, don't forget to fetch the milk."

"All right," she replied while chopping the potatoes. Giving them to her mother, she came out of the kitchen. In the bedroom, she stood in front of the long mirror her mother had brought along as a bride, took off the gamosa and fanned out her wet hair. A few drops of water trickled down. Her nostrils took in the familiar smell of shampoo and the freshness of wet hair mixed together. Whenever she dried her hair like this, she felt Bondeep's presence next to her. He often said, "When will I be able to sink my nose in your wet hair?" His words sent a small electric current through her breast. Bondeep talked about his desire to smell her bare body fresh from a bath, like he would a fragrant flower. When she first heard him say this she cringed, blushing with shyness. She trembled for some time afterwards like the taut string of a Veena that somebody tried to play on before letting it go.

She smelled her hair again. She also wanted that at such moments Bondeep would stand close to her and with his thirsty heart drink in the jasmine perfume of her hair. She wanted to hear the same words from him and feel the trembling of a string of her heart's veena. And as always, soft dreams would swirl around her, singing a chorus, as if in rhythm with the swaying Kahua flowers of autumn.

"Pari, if the pressure cooker whistles, switch it off. I am off with breakfast for your bordeuta."

Her mother's voice broke through her dream world. She smiled at her own foolishness; what made her lose herself in this kind of sentimentality from time to time? For Bondeep too, was there any value to these sentiments? The feelings that bloom for one another at first wilt slowly with time. She often went through Bondeep's old letters. Her old lovelorn beau lay supine in the pages she regarded as the best gift in her life.

She jumped at the whistle of the pressure cooker. The wet gamosa was still in her hand. She now went to the kitchen to switch off the stove and stepped out with the jug to collect the milk. It was not a job she liked to do because it had often brought her face to face with an unpleasant scene.

Ever since her childhood, Paridhi had witnessed astonishing changes coming over people she was familiar with. Her father, of course, was different. He was always the way she knew him: uncouth, a drunkard, insensitive, cruel. But Joydev was not like that. The great change in him introduced Paridhi to a strange colour of human life. There was a time when everybody in the village admired the young man; he was someone who had the imagination to dream of the wide sky even while looking through a hole in the roof in his cottage. His father died before he passed out of high school. A farmer, his father cultivated others' fields on a crop-sharing arrangement. He could not leave behind anything other than a hut with a roof that had holes in it on a small plot of land. Even then, Joydev's mother dreamt of a bright future for her son. Abject poverty could not chip away at that dream's beautiful image. Her Joydev would go to college, he would be a graduate. To help that dream come true she laboured day and night weaving clothes. When she designed the flowers on the mekhela-sador she often thought to herself—ah, let my Joydev get a job and then I'll welcome home a hard-working, nice girl as my daughter-in-law and after that I'll at last find time to take some rest. She met the household expenses and the cost of Joydev's school books by selling the clothes and even managed to save some money. That little fund was enough to brighten her dreams.

Ah, if people's lives could retain the same colours as their dreams!

Paridhi had heard about these things from the neighbours. When she was in school in a lower class, Joydev was already a grown-up. After graduation, he got a job as a clerk in some office in town. She was convinced that he was a very happy man because his fair face always wore a bright smile. She heard from others that he was like this ever since his childhood. His ever-smiling face did not betray that his belly was empty. Anyway, once he got the job, the state of his house improved slowly. Even if the house was made of reed and bamboo with a thatched roof, he brought many new things to fill it up. His mother tasted things that were foreign to her so far—cashew nuts, kismis, Horlicks, cornflakes. She was pleased to describe all these things to people she knew, praising her son to high heaven. A sense of pride overwhelmed her. She did not care that sometimes people were bored listening to the same adulatory talk about her great son. Meanwhile, the thatched roof of the house was replaced by a tin one. This change made the villagers comment, "Good, at last his mother's long days of suffering have borne fruit."

Paridhi waited near the iron gate and looked fearfully at

the front verandah, checking if Joydev was lying there stark naked. Thank God, there was no one there. She walked through the gate slowly and standing at the doorway called out to Joydev's mother, "Borma, Borma!" The woman responded from behind the house. She was washing clothes and asked her to wait. Paridhi had so many things to do today, she was impatient to leave. More than that, she was afraid to wait long in this courtyard. She was afraid of Joydev. That Joydev-da who hugged her fondly calling her his little sister, she was scared of him now. Who won't be after seeing a full grown man lying naked on the front verandah in broad daylight?

People now often talked about his unruly behaviour. He did not stop drinking at any time of the day. When he was like this, he yelled loudly to disturb the peace of the neighbourhood. He did not even spare his mother, attacking her with the choicest abuses. Young women, daughters-in-law of the houses next to his, pretended not to hear those words and quietly escaped from the presence of elderly relatives. Mothers trembled worrying if their young children would imitate those cuss words. Nobody knew when, why, or how, Joydev slid down to this state. Some said, he was in love with a girl but her father refused to give her hand to him because he was of a lower caste. Some said too much money went to his head. When a man coming from dismal poverty suddenly sees more money than expected, this is sure to happen.

Paridhi did not like these comments, but she believed

that this was what could have happened to Joydev. People these days were so enamoured by the madness of acquiring money and a luxurious life that they failed to appreciate the better things of life. They lost their way, unable to make a difference between the ascending and descending paths.

Joydev had managed to replace his dilapidated cottage with a concrete one within a very short time. The villagers looked up to him. He donated handsomely to the funds to celebrate Bihu, Durga puja and the *raas-bhaona* performances, where people enacted Lord Krishna and Radha's love story. He went around with a beautifully woven gamosa adorning his neck, presented by the grateful villagers. Those who saw past the façade of the concrete house, of the things he filled the interiors with for comfort, saw that Joydev had accomplished his goals through unethical means. He also started drinking. But his mother did not caution him. After all, he brought in lots of money and ensured a comfortable life for her. How could she say no to his little indulges? Paridhi was angry when she heard all this. She knew quite well how drinking could kill a man bit by bit. Nobody had to explain to her how the vile habit also affected a household. Wasn't her father the best example of it? She had witnessed many families on the rise who were destroyed by this addiction. She also heard a rumour that it was Joydev's mother who had objected to the girl Joydev loved and balked at welcoming her as a daughter-in-law. Who could say if the woman enjoying the new-found luxuries was wary of bringing in another person to the household? If her son gave too much attention to his new bride, wouldn't she lose out on this well-appointed lifestyle, earned after years of poverty?

Joydev was quite loquacious by nature but he never confided in anyone. His drinking increased. One day he was pulled up by the Additional Deputy Commissioner for coming to the office drunk. Bereft of any sense, Joydev was incensed enough to raise his hand on his boss. Naturally, he was sacked, and he started drinking more. His savings depleted quickly. His mother thought of buying a cow with her savings and start a business of selling milk. She had long given up weaving clothes and now, with her weakened eyes that needed high-powered glasses, it was not possible either.

Though Paridhi sympathised with Joydev's inner turmoil, she was irritated too. She could not accept that he opted to live a lavish life built on corruption. His face, which was open and handsome once, now seemed ugly to her. Remembering the incident she almost stopped breathing.

That particular day, opening the gate as she entered, she found Joydev without a stitch on him; at first, she almost thought it was a ghost. He sat on the stairwell with his back to her, his weight resting on his elbows, his eyes closed and face upturned. She did not know if he saw her, but she ran out in fear. She ran and ran. Only after reaching home could she take a long breath. She told her mother what she had seen. Her mother said that she too had heard about it from others. One day, when villagers saw him like that by the roadside, they threw some clothes on his bare body and dragged him home.

"Be careful, Pari! If you see him by himself, don't enter the house at all. If I could manage to get some milk elsewhere I would have stopped buying milk from them. But I am helpless. I need the milk for your bordeuta's breakfast and afternoon tea."

Her forehead showed a million wrinkles bunched together as she said it.

That night Paridhi had a strange dream. The milk from her jug spilled on the floor; the white milk slowly turned red like wine and a naked man hunched like a cat over it, slurping it up .

"Here, give me the jug!" Paridhi jumped up hearing Joydev's mother addressing her.

"What were you thinking about?"

"No, nothing important. Here, Borma! I'm in a hurry today."

She walked fast homeward as soon as Joydev's mother filled the jug. Once the woman started talking Paridhi would be stuck. She still made an effort to talk about her son in a salutary manner pretending that there was nothing amiss. Paridhi was aware about this habit some people had; even if time withered away colour from the mind, they did not stop painting their faces for outward appearance.

5

Paridhi was lying on the bed in the dark room and listening to songs on the music system. Bondeep had recently presented it to her. Though they were close, she felt somewhat hesitant to accept expensive gifts from him. It was her own angst, of course. Though her love for him made her concede, in such instances it disturbed her sense of pride too. Bondeep was annoyed at her attitude. He even commented that she was 'too proud' sometimes. Paridhi retaliated by asking why he confused self-respect with ego. He too did not mince his words and said, "So you think I am not close to you? Maybe you don't. Otherwise, you wouldn't have behaved like this."

Sometimes, the exchange of innocuous words between lovers suddenly flare up to create misunderstandings. One blames the other for the situation. Then follows tears, perhaps threats of committing suicide; both stop talking to each other—a stalemate in a duel. Yes, a game indeed.

When Paridhi was in such a conundrum, the days and

nights seemed to stretch on. She sulked silently. She even wondered if it would have been better if she had not fallen in love at all. Love could be like the delicate wings of a butterfly. Sometimes they were pierced by the sharp thorns of a cactus. At such times she felt that nobody understood her—even the man most intimate to her. The intensity of this unhappiness enveloped all other mental distresses. Her fingers hovered on the keys of the phone to send an SMS, but pride made her pause.

This state ended with Bondeep's message, "Please forgive me, my heart! I love you!"

Suddenly the soft wings ripped by thorns magically repaired themselves.

Still lying down, she increased the volume of the music with the remote control button. In the half-darkness of the bolted room, soft music created an intimate atmosphere.

What stories the river carries with her waves...who is in its secret thoughts...

Who else would be in her thoughts? Songs reflect feelings in the deepest core of the heart, isn't it? For ages they have been talking about life and its many facets. Even an ancient pain that lies hidden somewhere emerges with the strains of a song. That's why, when sadness overtook Paridhi she took solace in songs that talked about deep yearning.

The distant stars peep, my sorrow lies hidden deep
I feel so alone...so alone...why it feels like this today...

Paridhi lost herself in the music. Keshab Mahanta's

lyrics and Papon singing in the bhatiyali overtones of boatmen. The day's tiredness, combined with the beauty of the music now made her feel drowsy. She wanted to be cut off from the world outside and just listen to the songs, lost in a dream world.

But she did not have the luxury of being left alone for long. Her mother knocked on the door. Paridhi liked to lock the door when she wanted to listen to music in a dark room. Her mother often complained, "You can just shut the door; why do you have to lock it?" How could she make her mother understand that at times it felt better to be cut off from the outside world? Reluctantly, she got up to open the door. Her mother immediately switched on the light. It pierced the darkness of the room unpleasantly.

"Your Shontu-dada called today," her mother informed her while giving her a cup of tea.

"Oh, really? What did he say?" Paridhi asked without showing much enthusiasm and sipped the tea.

Her mother was talking about Dipak. Shontu was his nick name. He was her bordeuta's eldest son. He was coming with his family to look up his father, her mother informed. He would come next Saturday and then return to the city on Monday. Paridhi did not pay much attention to her mother as she elaborated on her cousin's impending visit. Instead, her ears picked up the *hish…hish…* of the train on its return journey from Guwahati. A little later, the harsh sound of something scraping the track told her that the train was about to stop. A long whistle followed.

She heard the auto-rickshaws and tempo vans starting their engines for the passengers' commute. All of a sudden, Paridhi felt like going back to her half-written story. She did not finish her tea. Her mother left the room, taking the cup with her. If her mother asked her about something she did not hear. She switched off the music system, pulled out the chair of her desk and opened her writing pad.

From a very young age, perhaps she was four or five years old then, Paridhi remembered the old woman who dashed to the station at the sound of the whistle of an approaching train. From their corner of the village, at a stone's throw, was the locality where the people of the Tiwa community lived. In a ramshackle cottage there, an old widow stayed with her eldest son. Her younger son had married a girl who ran away from her home to be with her son. Soon, they arranged a separate kitchen for themselves. Her daughter had also run away with a man from Bihar who worked as a mason. To eke out a living, the woman took up chores like cleaning chaff from rice grains, sweeping and swabbing the floors in households in the village and so on. In exchange, besides the cash, kind householders often gave her some rice and pulses, even old mekhela-sador sets and blouses, that she could use.

While on her way to work, she often visited Paridhi's

house to enquire about her mother's well-being while enjoying the tamul paan, betel nut and leaf, offered to her. The betel nut in her mouth was always there and one could see two blood red lines dripping down from both sides of her lips. Matching the colour were her colourful stories of people in the village. Listening to her, sometimes her mother forgot that the vegetable curry was boiling in the wok. A burnt smell would waft from the kitchen to alert her; sometimes the rice got overcooked too and became sticky. Oh! When her father was served this food for lunch you should have seen the brouhaha. Paridhi trembled at the memory even now. At these times, she became angry with Tilottama jethai. Paridhi addressed her with the suffix jethai as her mother called the widow baideu respectfully, elder sister. Villagers called her Tilu bai, the baideu shortened to bai.

Tilu bai's house looked as if a thin old man ravaged by rheumatism was somehow trying to stand up. The thatched roof with gaps here and there looked like an old man's head with thinning grey hair. The woman must have had to put a bucket underneath the ceiling on rainy days.

Even Paridhi had to place a bucket on the floor beneath the ceiling when it rained. The house was constructed long ago and the tin roof and ceiling had holes here and there. Their house had an earthen floor and up on the ceiling there was a hard mud coating. Was her grandfather so much in love with earth? Her grandparents had died long before Paridhi was born. For her, they were just two entities in the framed photograph that was adorned with two dried bokul flower garlands. Sometimes she wondered why the man in the black-and-white photograph was so in love with clay, to the extent that the ceiling, woven with common bamboo and the scaffolding held together with wooden bits, was covered with a layer of thick earth. It was painted a light green.

Earth. Man. Colour.

Perhaps these three were entwined together forever. Perhaps her grandfather understood that earth is man's true friend and lover, the one who kept vigil on the body from birth till death and was ready to embrace it in the end.

Paridhi wanted to write a story on the life of a very ordinary woman like Tilottama jethai. Instead, she started reminiscing about her own childhood. Her thoughts flowed like an unbound river. They did not conform to the meaning of her name. Paridhi—limited, but reaching beyond borders.

By the time Paridhi grew up, the base of the sturdy sal timber posts that held up the frame of the house was getting invaded by termites. Small coves showed up on them. Once, Paridhi had pushed her hand inside one and then could not take it out. Her brother had to pull it out but the skin on her hand had been lacerated. Those holes were safe havens for rodents. Indeed, it's a never-ending fight for survival—be it insects, gecko, rats or men, all trying to find a safe place to live in.

Who is safe in this world?

The chunks of earth that fell off from the ceiling of their house, loosened due to age or shaken by the tremor of earthquakes frequent in these parts, reminded her that uncertainty was a part of life.

The singer Shuvomita's song jolted her out of her reminisces. Bondeep.

"Yes, tell me," her voice was tired.

"There's some good news, Ridhi!"

He sometimes called her by that name.

"What? Has your mother said anything?" Paridhi immediately perked up.

"Not really. I'm happy to share that Supriti baideu has agreed to publish her latest book with us."

Paridhi was disappointed. She had been expecting Bondeep's mother to give a green signal to their union. Even then, the news made her happy.

"That's great. The book which was serially published in the *Annashwan* magazine?" she asked.

"Yes, that's the one."

"It's really good. I love her descriptions. I always wait for the next instalment. How beautifully she has used fairy tales to merge into today's sensibilities."

Paridhi wanted to discuss the book. But Bondeep said, "We'll talk later," and ended the call abruptly.

He often did that these days. As soon as he finished what he wanted to say, he went off the line. Bondeep was too busy now trying to build a safe shelter, he didn't have time. Paridhi suppressed her rising temper and opened the window near the table. The moon hanging between the branches of the moringa tree was touched by a slice of dark cloud. Paridhi picked up the pen again.

As Tilottama's elder son grew up to be a young man, she did not have to work at people's houses anymore. He started his own business—he went to the market in Guwahati to sell homegrown vegetables. Papayas, colacasias, elephant apples, kath-alu yams, gourds, mint leaves, etc. He was not alone. A few other young men like him from the village also did the same. They packed the produce in sacks, carried them on their cycles and parked them at houses in the neighbourhood for the day. Then carrying the sacks on their shoulders, they crossed over to the railway station. Some parked their cycles at Paridhi's house too. For that her father charged money. It made her cringe in shame—what kind of man was he, squeezing money out of the poor?

Her father's habit of borrowing money whenever he got an opportunity troubled Paridhi no end. She felt guilty and ashamed in front of other people. Not that her uncle did not give his brother any money. He did. But her father soon spent it on alcohol. That's why her mother begged him not to give money to her husband. Giving heed to her plea, one day, when her uncle refused to give money to his brother, he abused him. The astute man tried his best to cool him down, but he did not listen and at last he had to give up. Then her father did the unthinkable; he insinuated, even though the children were around, that his elder brother and his wife were having an affair. Her mother covered her face in utter shame and disappeared into the inner quarters immediately. And her bordeuta, how did he react? He stood there as if he had turned into stone.

Paridhi was too young to express herself but even then she understood with bitterness what it meant to be born to an unworthy man.

At times, she too felt that it was better to be turned into a stone. Not once but many times on different occasions. She prayed for another Maharshi Gautam, the sage, to appear before her and curse her and turn her into a stone as he did to Ahalya. It would not be a misfortune, she thought, it would be a blessing.

Looking at the pebbles painted with birds, fish, tortoise, red and blue ladybirds, human faces, and Lord Ganapati in different poses, Mayur had commented once, "They could be some beings from another time who turned into stones. Some sage might have cursed them; now in your hand they have found a new life."

Paridhi liked that idea too. Perhaps these pebbles were parts of Ahalya, Maharshi Gautam's wife and daughter of King Mudgala. What was her son's name? Paridhi tried to remember. Satananda. Yes, Satananda.

Paridhi could not recall exactly when her interest in painting on stones began. Some years ago, Rupak, her uncle's younger son, had gone on a picnic to Bhalukpung at the Arunachal border and brought back a handful of pebbles from the Jia Bharali River flowing there. He had confessed that he did not know why he walked to a distance from the picnic spot and collected the stones from the bank. At first, she just enjoyed running her fingers over the smooth surface of the stones but did not feel any special attraction to them. The big basket where the stones were kept was placed in a corner amidst the paraphernalia on the teakwood cot going back to her grandmother's time. Sometimes a visitor would take one of them to use as a pestle, while someone else took away another attracted by its beauty. So the stones denuded away slowly. The rest were lying neglected in a corner. But once Paridhi started painting on them, they emerged with their own personalities and soon found a place in the drawing room to be displayed as decorative pieces.

There was a wheat-coloured, oval one weighing almost as much as a mature melon. Visitors to their house often looked at it curiously. When little children were told that it was the egg of a dinosaur, they believed her. Though it was quite heavy, Rupak did not leave it behind on that picnic trip. People often asked how he carried it along so far. Paridhi wanted to turn it into a bird. She drew a white bird on the surface, its wings spread and ready to fly.

"A bird of stone," she uttered the words to herself once the painting was done.

Even now it was there in a corner of the drawing room, its dream of flying somewhere still unfulfilled.

Paridhi had heard many fables about stone figures. She often remembered the story of Phulara and Satala at the juncture of the Manah and Luit rivers. They were still there, turned into stone by some sage's curse. Nabaneeta had told her about the huge stone to the west of Baromboi hill near Hajo, famous for rocks. According to legend the stream that flowed over the stone symbolised the tears of a newlywed couple. When they were walking by the Baromboi hill, a fierce storm suddenly blew in. They took shelter in a cave behind the stone. But a sudden earthquake made a huge stone tumble down from above; it closed the mouth of the cave. The poor couple could never come out. And thus, the huge stone, always wet, turned into a fable.

In fact, stones are unending sources of stories in Assam. Kamakhya, Basistha, Aswaklanta, Umananda, Hajo, Haigrib—all of these pilgrimage centres have carried stories of their own for eons. They say that at the Chand-dinga temple in Dhubri there is a black stone which nobody has ever been able to lift. According to legends, the merchant Chand Saudagar's boat had rammed against it. Lakhindar's father, Chand Saudagar, had refused to pray to the Snake Goddess Manasa and he had to pay the price; all his six sons died of snake-bite. Even though he locked up his seventh son, Lakhindar, and Behula in an impregnable stone house on their wedding night, the goddess still found a way to get in. Behula sailed on a boat down the Brahmaputra with Lakhindar's dead body to reach the gods to beg for her husband's life and succeeded.

The two stones at Bordowa and Rangajan carry the images of the soles of Mahapurush Sankardev and his disciple Madhabdev who were at the helm of the Vaishnavite movement in Assam.

And then there is the bor-shil, the big stone, on the border of Assam and Nagaland. It is witness to the love story of Ahom king, Gadadhar, and the Naga maiden, Dalimi. Gadadhar was ousted by his rivals from the capital and when in exile, he fell in love with Dalimi who looked after him. Gadadhar's name is also associated with his devoted wife, Joymoti, who was tortured to death as she refused to reveal his whereabouts to his enemies. Later, Gadadhar had his revenge and was reinstated as a powerful king.

Somehow all these stories about stones stirred Paridhi. Mayur was right in calling her the 'Stone Princess'.

Yes, the stories of the Water Princess that coloured her imagination once were now replaced by stories about stones.

On the bank of the Brahmaputra, near Silghat, there are two rocky hills; they look like two meditating munis, sages. People call them dui muni sila, that is, a duo of *munis*. Even during the high monsoon when the river overflows, the two heads of the rocks never get submerged, people say.

Paridhi had heard the story of the pair of hills from her uncle.

King Baan of Tezpur was planning to build a replica of Kashi at Biswanath in his kingdom by the Brahmaputra. So he sat in tapasya, seeking blessings from Lord Shiva.

Pleased with Baan's devotion, the Lord gave him a boon. The king selected a place stretching from Bhomoraguri hill to Silghat, called it Kanyashram and set up a hundred crore Shiva-lingas. But the gods were not willing to accept another Kashi beyond Varanasi. However, Lord Shiva, unaware of the others' resentment, had already granted the king the boon. Now, nothing could be done about it. They were helpless. Meanwhile, Lord Ganesh hid one of the lingas. King Baan searched everywhere because he had to have the right number. So he sat to meditate again to pray to Lord Shiva. When Shiva appeared again before him, Baan told him about the missing Shiva-linga. Shiva said that he should approach the two sages, Kumud and Kaustav, who were meditating at Kanyashram and they would guide him. On arrival at Kanyasharam, Baan, arrogant as he was, shouted "Where is Kashi?" The munis were in deep meditation; they lost their temper at being disturbed and gave him a dressing down. Insulted, Baan was ready to commit suicide, but Lord Shiva appeared in front of his bhakt. The king explained to him why he was ready to take this extreme step. At that, Shiva also got incensed and rebuked the two rishis: "If you don't have patience what kind of sages are you? Go turn into stones!" So Kumud and Kaustav turned into two hillocks. According to the fable, only a war of seven mlechha would free them and they could turn to humans again.

In the mythical story, Shiva said, 'there would be a war among seven barbarians (mlechha) to the Dikrang river's east during the end of Kaliyug. Blood of dead soldiers, elephants etc. would flow in the river.

Sometimes human beings turn into stones. But could stones turn back into humans beings? These questions often ran through Paridhi's disturbed mind. Sometimes one needed to become hard like a stone to survive in life.

What indeed had she not seen in her short life?

She had seen people fed up with life, denying their own existence and then turning into living stones. She had seen people going stiff like fish craving water on a riverbank. Her eyes had absorbed their stories like blotting paper sucking in ink.

Some readers praised Paridhi's stories a lot. If they happened to meet her for the first time they commented, "From your stories we were under the impression that you were more than 40 years old." She was not ready to believe them. Was she really able to narrate like a mature writer? She was, after all, still learning. Her life, hanging between light and darkness, and the people around her, were the inspiration behind her writing. When the soft or distressed voices from the world around called out to her and she could not ignore them, she took up the pen or the paint brush. Sometimes she found herself extremely helpless. Like many, she too was perhaps a dumb witness to this hell on earth.

Every other second, news of someone turning into stone, of bloodshed, of the body turning into merely a lump of flesh reach every corner of the room. Nobody knows when, at what moment, one could become a 'news clip'.

Tilottama's son used to travel by the morning train at 7 o'clock to Guwahati and return at about 8.30 pm. But one day, he did not come back. Tilottama waited at the gate with the almost dying tipsaki, a small hand lamp. She waited and waited and waited till that night became the next…and then the next. After a while, she quit waiting at the gate. As soon as she heard the whistle of a train she ran towards the station like a mad woman. There was no one to hold her back. The villagers were apprehensive that the way she ran on the road at any time of the night, she could accidentally be killed by a vehicle. To tell the truth, Paridhi secretly wished for her death. She was surprised at her own callousness, but it was true. She had not seen a ghost in real life, but she had seen real people become like ghosts. To her, Tilu jethai looked like one of them. So she prayed that by whatever means, the woman be set free from this excruciatingly painful existence.

Perhaps Tilottama's son had also become a news item. But at that time there was no swift electronic media to carry the message of someone found turning into stone in a jungle, or a blood-soaked lump on a city street in these troubled times.

6

The crimson sun was hanging uncertainly in the sky on the other side of the field. It painted the field in a jetuka leaf hue. Small posies of cloud floated in the sky. In the distance, a cluster of clouds looked like a horse ready to gallop.

Paridhi's eyes followed the slowly descending sun. It would be dark soon and blot out the warm henna colour the field was awash in. The trees and plants would hide their lush green in the dark for the time being. Soon the earth would lose its vibrancy. Black does not compromise, it envelops. Witness to the ugliness of life from a young age, though a part of Paridhi's mind was veiled in darkness, the other part still looked out for the glory of colour.

Perhaps it was the power of colour, Paridhi often thought. It still found a way to escape through a hole even if a door was shut tight.

After a long time, she had come to the railway station. She did not sit on the stone bench but walked ahead.

The wooden bench had disappeared. Perhaps the wood had rotted. In its place was an iron bench painted in white. Paridhi sat down there. The morning was spent at the keyboard of the computer and she was tired. Now the silence of the afternoon and its mellow golden light rejuvenated her. She liked talking to herself in a silent soliloquy whenever she got an opportunity like this. At such moments, her thoughts travelled in a wide arc. Earlier, she would have talked to Bondeep on the phone at such lonely times. But now it seemed that there was nothing to talk about; all that had to be said had been said and heard.

Perhaps conversations between lovers are often like this—changing contours with time. The intense passion words created between them at first, some of them said, some left unsaid, had now cooled down. Yet, there remained something of a bond between them. Maybe it was love.

Paridhi looked at the setting sun again. Before saying farewell to the day how gorgeously it painted the sky, as if it was a parting gift.

Even a farewell can be so vibrant. What else can have that power?

People? They go away too, but leave behind traces of their existence in one's heart.

What if Bondeep left her? Or, what if he had to go away? Even the possibility made her tremble, as if shaken by a mild earthquake. But she knew that even if Bondeep had changed a bit in recent times, or he had less time for her, he could not possibly leave her. Because he loved her. Period.

There was no doubt there. But time sometimes imprisoned men in stone fortresses. Sure, she had full faith that he had the strength to break through its confines. Yet, she did not know why doubts sprang in her mind like the pervasive sokamora weeds in the paddy fields sometimes. Whenever Paridhi thought about their relationship, a house of their own in a plot of land, the face of a middle-aged woman, fair in complexion, her forehead adorned with a sandalwood paste spot appeared in her mind simultaneously.

Bondeep's mother.

She was not happy about their relationship. How could she, a Brahmin, think of welcoming a daughter-in-law from a lower caste shudir family? Paridhi felt her blood boil at such antiquated attitudes. When she heard these things, even though she tried to respect the woman who was her beloved's mother, she could not bring herself to do it. She knew that it was not wholly the elderly lady's fault. She was also the product of a society that encouraged such narrow-mindedness. She was apprehensive that if Paridhi entered the household, she would have to face the ire of her community. To defy the diktat of society, one has to have the mental strength and adequate belief which few can muster. In this case, it was obviously missing.

There was always someone out there obstructing in the path of somebody else's dreams, Paridhi realised it early in her life. In a way, it's man who brings darkness to fellow man, not external natural factors.

Sitting on the bench of the platform and looking at

the horizon where the sun was ready to depart for the day, these same thoughts troubled Paridhi again. Juroni was not by her side, but she did not miss her. Sometimes she liked to sit by herself. In the utter silence she thought she could often hear nature's lullaby, a song she never heard from anyone but her mother.

That day she cried her heart out sitting alone. Drained now, she looked once again at the sun. She had an intense desire to address it as deuta, her father. She remembered how her father tore her paint book and the way her heart shook with sorrow. It felt as if he had not just torn her book of paintings, but he had torn at her soul. She did not know why, despite his repeated abuses and warnings, she still took up the coloured pencils instead of the pen. Her fingers travelled here and there drawing lines and filled the pages in many hues. She tried to imagine things she had seen around her and interpreted them in her own way to make them vibrant. She did not know the language of a trained painter. But it was through the medium of paintings that a desire to live took tentative steps inside her despite her father's irrational cruelty.

Sometimes she felt a thirst that dried her soul. She ran to get some water and sprinkled it on a bare page. Then let her fingers dipped in colour move aimlessly over it. At these moments, all the shades of life gathered in her heart. Her parched lips found moisture. But for her father, these were unnecessary luxuries and meaningless expenses.

"Forget all this stupidity. Our kind doesn't have room

for artists. No, I won't allow this nonsense in my house. From today if I see this business of so-called painting, you'll see what I'll do. I warn too the one who buys you these things."

The last sentence was spoken more loudly so that it reached her uncle's ears.

Her father just needed an excuse to create a ruckus. Her neighbours were also privy to his yelling. The genteel folk in the village, did they look at their house with contempt as the house of a drunkard? Did they look askance at Paridhi and Paras because they were children of an alcoholic father? All these thoughts made young Paridhi cringe in shame and self-doubt.

She did not know how Paras reacted to this terrible situation. He slowly became more and more introverted. People in such a state of mind are supposed to have a sea of feelings hidden inside, she read somewhere. Paridhi did not have an opportunity to fathom the depth of that sea. Her brother was on the threshold of youth. Lately, he hardly spent any time at home. Now his passion was theatre instead of cinema. With a group of boys from the village, he travelled around other villages and staged theatre performances.

But where could Paridhi go? She was yet to develop the spine to cock a snook at her father and go out, like a man, whenever she wanted and seek solace in the lap of nature. She did not have the gumption either to protest when, as she and Juroni sat on the bench of the platform talking, a few rogues sitting on the railway track called to them with innuendoes while smoking bidis. It took time to be more assertive.

But even now, was she that strong? Had she become unyielding like a stone that could not be broken into pieces by someone? Had she been able to stand up with a voice, strong and loud, against the injustice of people? She was not sure how much strength life's experiences had helped her build, but an immovable tree she was not. But yes, the girl who once could not utter a single hard word would not stand silently now if she encountered bias and discrimination. For whatever reason, she felt sad when the word 'human' got sullied. What made her feel most desolate was when she saw a man sinking to a level that could not be called human.

"Hei Pari-ba, what are you doing here sitting alone?"

Paridhi almost jumped up. She turned her head to see who it was. Rekhamoni.

"When did you come?"

"Day before yesterday. Sorry, I haven't been able to visit you yet."

"Oh, don't bother. Why should you come?" Paridhi replied, obviously piqued.

Till she got married, Rekhamoni, three years younger to her and a neighbour, was always hovering around her. When she went to the market Paridhi often took her along too. Rekhamoni was fond of reading and often borrowed books from her. True, she could not pass her Matriculation exam, but she could empathise with the characters and plots in novels and short stories. She was the one who told Paridhi one day, "Why is it that good people suffer so much? Whether in films, TV serials or books—they always show good people suffering in the end."

Paridhi was convinced that Rekhamoni was married off too young.

"Why are you offended, Ba? I come here after such a long gap but as soon as I arrive, I have to enter the kitchen. We are like the dhenki, the grinding pestle; whether on earth or in heaven, the work is the same. My mother is not well. Anyway, I'll come to your house tomorrow. Hope you'll be at home?"

Paridhi assured her that she would be. Rekhamoni enquired after the well-being of the other members in the house.

Paridhi was meeting Rekhamoni after a long time. Even then, her face with a red dot on her forehead now, seemed a little altered. Where was that vivacious girl? Did she still nurture her love of books? Rekhamoni was talking nineteen to the dozen but half of them did not register with Paridhi. She was examining her intensely.

Many years ago, she and Rekhamoni sat exactly at this spot and discussed the characters in books they both admired. Chandan-Champa, Arunav-Anuradha, Binapani, Varsha, Kanchan, Satyabati, Suvarna, Bokul—characters they ruminated on again and again.

"Do you still read books?" Paridhi asked.

Rekhamoni was hesitant as she replied, "It's difficult to find time, and I don't have access to books too."

This girl, years younger to her, was now a woman with the full responsibility of running a household. She was also the mother of a four-year-old son. Would her husband spare her if she took herself off from household chores and indulged in reading books, Paridhi thought sardonically.

"You know, we don't even get a newspaper to read there. One day I found a few issues of the *Bismoy* magazine on my younger brother-in-law's table and tried to read but my mother-in-law was very unhappy and didn't spare me with her words. Oh, what a hole I have entered!"

Paridhi remembered that at one time Rekhamoni hummed a few lines of song often:

The beaks of Kamsarai bird are red
There I put a vermillion spot
O my mother, O my father
Please don't marry me off to a far-off place

Rekhamoni had come to the station to buy misol, a mixture of savoury bites served in paper packets. On one side of the platform a young boy was shouting, inviting customers with baro misol, tero swad–buy a dozen misol, get the taste of thirteen. They went to check on the offering. Rekhamoni bought two and gave one to Paridhi.

"Oh, I was dying to have it. My mother told me it's sold here. She told me even meat is available here now. In a way it's good, people don't have to go to the four-road junction, the chariali, to get it," Rekhamonui said.

"Yes, that's right. But there are other things sold too. Coming here in the evening is rather risky. The atmosphere is not good. As soon as evening sets in, groups of boys, adolescents and youth, descend. Alcohol, charas, gambling—you name it, everything is available. Somebody said one day a woman's bra was found lying here. Of course, I didn't see it, only heard."

"Why doesn't the station master object?" Rekhamoni was shocked.

"Oh, he has. Quite a few times. But they threatened him and so fearing for his life, he stopped. After all, he has a young daughter too and it's natural that he would be scared. Not everybody can be a film hero. If Paras were here perhaps it would have been different. He and his friends tried hard to stop the bhati-khana, from functioning. They didn't even care for their lives. They were successful too. But..." Paridhi's voice filled with unshed tears.

Rekhamoni put her hand on her shoulder.

Paras went away. His friends too were not in the village anymore. The need to make a living drew them to the town. After they left, the business of the brewery flourished again. And it continued; nobody even thought of demolishing the brewery. These days, people did not care that the young boys and spineless men of the village were getting addicted to alcohol. Once, Paridhi went to meet a few senior people and educated young men of the village with the idea of shutting down the brewery. At first, all seemed to agree that it was necessary but afterwards, nobody came forward.

When she saw men walking unsteadily on the road in front of her house, anger and frustration overtook her. The pain of not being able to do anything about it upset her no end.

Slowly, the henna-coloured late afternoon merged into the soft darkness of early evening. The station was lit up by electric lights. The windows of the quarters next to it also glowed now. When they were young, there were no electric lights here. As soon as evening fell the assistant of the station master lit up two kerosene lamps. One of them was placed in the ticket counter room and another was hung from a hook on the verandah. Sure, the pale light of the lamp was not adequate, but nobody thought of taking advantage of the dim light either for nefarious activities.

Still chatting with Rekhamoni, Paridhi walked towards her house. She looked at the field beyond once again. The darkness that the station-lights chased away from the station seemed to gather there as if finding a safe shelter.

7

Rekhamoni kept her word. She came to visit her next morning. She also brought along a few sticks of moringa from the bunch she carried for her parents from the kitchen garden of her marital home. Rekhamoni spent quite a long time with Paridhi even though she kept saying that she should leave now. After she had tea and snacks and paan, Paridhi gave her two novels that she guessed could be to her taste.

"Even women who work at others' houses find time to write a book; you can at least put aside some time to read books which you love. Ashapurna Devi used to write every day before retiring to bed at night. I am sure you can read at least during that period."

She paused a bit before adding, "Your husband is often away from home for work, isn't it? Ok, I understand, you don't have to read when he is around."

Rekhamoni smiled at Paridhi and accepted the books as if they were prasad offered from the temple. She held them to her chest and went to the kitchen to bid goodbye to Paridhi's mother. Paridhi accompanied her as she went to the verandah to meet her uncle who was sitting there and touched his feet to seek his blessing before she left.

As she bid goodbye, Paridhi reminded her, "You may live in a remote village but if you have books with you the window to the world will always remain open."

"Thank you, Pari-ba. I'll surely read. At night before going to bed. I'll keep my window open. I'll take more books from you next time I am here," Rekhamoni shouted from the road on her way home. Paridhi smiled.

Back in her room she checked her phone as a matter of habit.

"Thanks Paridhi!" Nabaneeta's message.

Paridhi had not checked her Facebook page for the last few days. As she opened it now, the Inbox came alive with many messages entering like noisy children in a classroom. Reluctantly she read the messages. Most of them were inane, like, 'Hi!', 'Hello!', 'How are you?', 'Have you had lunch? 'What are you doing now?' She did not find them worth responding to. She clicked on Nabaneeta's message again. She had sent the story as soon as she had finished it. Paridhi sent her a smiley emoji in acknowledgment. Now she clicked on Bondeep's profile to check if there were any updates. She also checked the comments on his status. Why was she so interested? Sometimes she teased Bondeep about some comment from a female admirer. She also had a little grouse around his Facebook posts. Earlier, she was the first reader of his poems or the first sentence of a poetic description. Since he met her, she was the one to whom he read out his observations about people, the world or life in general. But these days, many of his thoughts to which she was yet to be privy were there on his Facebook page already. She felt abandoned. The man she knew so well seemed like a stranger on Facebook. Were there many other things about him which she was unaware of? She typed on the mobile, "These days you seem to do very well without me." Immersed in work, the sudden message bewildered Bondeep and he replied, "Why are you saying this, my love?" Paridhi did not reply. Given his long association with her, he should have been able to guess that sometimes a woman's silence is portent of a storm ahead.

Facebook! What a thing that has come up, Paridhi often mused. Like a glass bubbling with possibilities. While immersed in this 'book' what was it that people actually read? Do they try to gauge the real people behind the faces? Or, get a glimpse of their hidden feelings? What were the things one read in this book? For those absorbed in the book perhaps everything seemed fine, hunky-dory. Ah, what a good book it was. You could reach so many people at the click of a finger and even reconnect with long-lost people. There was no room for loneliness here. Even when super-busy, for a moment you could forget your tiredness, irritation or sadness. No need to move from the chair, just a few taps on the keyboard to share your thoughts, your happiness, even your sorrow. In exchange you got a certain kind of satisfaction. Through this window you saw how the world outside rotates—and the people.

So many faces...

Sometimes Paridhi was amazed how, like the stars in the evening sky, the number of 'friends' increased. In hundreds, in thousands. Could anybody see the real colour beneath those facades? Perhaps busy proclaiming themselves, people did not even want to see them. What mattered was the colour that came alive easily at a touch of a finger, lulling them into self-satisfaction.

True, the days when she hid herself underneath the bed, trembling, were long gone. That person, always livid, whose eyes were like burning cinders, was not there anymore. He had expired. Now she had an open courtyard to herself where she could play with colours without fear. The house was not full of luxuries but there was enough to live comfortably. She was surrounded by people who gave her a sense of peace and security. Even then, why was she still apprehensive? Despite having someone by her side whom she loved dearly. Yet this feeling of loneliness engulfed her periodically. Why did it feel like this? Or was it because, as Bondeep observed, she liked to wallow in melancholy she herself had brought on? Was she piqued at small things more than necessary? Or was she weak? Perhaps that thin, insecure, adolescent girl was still there somewhere inside the woman that she was now—one who was determined to grow up into a strong tree with its roots going deep into the earth.

Perhaps Paridhi was forever fearful of losing something. The memory of the story of the water princess did not leave her. None of the stories that Juroni's mother narrated had a happy ending.

What had happened to the water princess who was so in love with Nabakumar?

Even while swimming she yearned for something else and later kept sitting on the big rock on the bank of the pond. When she saw Nabakumar from a distance, she moved her tail seductively. She was supposed to have drawn him down to the water and he returned fulfilled. Only when she grew up did Paridhi understand why his body smelled of fish. Jayanti-khuri did not reveal the secret because they were too young to hear it.

Days passed happily like this. But one day, Nabakumar found his princess wasn't there at their meeting place. He sat on the stone slab hoping to see her. He sat through the whole day but returned home disappointed. Nabakumar waited and waited. His body shrunk as if starved of food. One day, the villagers found him lying there unconscious. His eyes were flat, almost deathly, and a blue tinge covered his face. He was naked. His body was covered with fish scales.

Suddenly, Paridhi felt her throat go dry. Should she call Bondeep? No, she wouldn't. If he could go without hearing from her this long, she could too. Did she fool herself into believing in something that was not there? Most people perhaps did. A few days ago, while reading

Manik Bandopadhyay's novel *Putul Nacher Itikatha,* she had marked out a few lines with a pencil. They went something like this: 'People in general deceive themselves. Those who try to analyse events in life face sorrow. So those who question should not expect much from life. More the expectations, more the disappointments.'

Even in moments when she was happily submerged in a world of colours, hard truths nudged at her. Sometimes their presence was intense enough to dislodge her equilibrium. In such moments, Paridhi's dreams seemed to empty out from her soul. Sleep lost its way to her eyes. The thoughts went up and down like waves in her brain and tired her out. She asked herself, repeating as before—what is it that I want?

Sometimes the question disturbed her so much that a powerful desire to run away somewhere overcame her. She then remembered the homeless people she met in her childhood.

Yes, homeless people.

She saw herself now, walking by the narrow lane in the shadow of bamboo trees. She did not know where or why. Following Juroni seemed to be the only logical thing to do. From the field beyond the lane, a cacophony of voices reached them.

"Why have you brought me here?" Paridhi asked, unable to keep quiet.

"Come, walk on! You'll find out soon," Juroni said, unwilling to give in easily. She wanted to maintain the suspense. So they walked silently, their feet crunching the fallen leaves. At the end of the lane, they found the source of the voices.

There were about ten to fifteen people. Their eyes were fixed on something. Following their line of sight, Paidhi saw something that made her cringe. A smell that seemed familiar invaded her nostrils.

"What's that?"

"Johamal," somebody said from the crowd. The animal exuded the sweet fragrance of Joha rice.

The animal looked like a cat but its body was longer, its mouth sharper. A black stripe ran over its back. The long furry tail was marked in segments of black and white. Was it sleeping? No, the soft body with the black and white fur seemed still. There was blood oozing from its neck. It mixed with the dirt and looked murky. On the furry body a thin, jet-black hand ran up and down from the head to its tail. The nails on the fingers were unusually white.

With skin dark as coal and sunken yellow eyes, the man looked strange. His hair was rough, dry and tangled. Perhaps it had never been introduced to a comb. As he ran his hand tenderly over the dead animal's body on the ground, a group of similar looking men sat around him, watching. Paridhi's eyes travelled from one person to another. The ribs in their emaciated bodies stood out. Their upper torsos were bare. The lower portions were wrapped in dirty lungis.

"How did they kill him? What will they do with it

now? Where have they come from?" The questions floated around as the villagers wondered aloud. There was that unmistakable smell of aromatic Joha rice wafting in the air.

The men were deep in discussion among themselves in a language the villagers did not understand. One of the strangers searched for something in the patchwork sack that was hanging from his shoulder. There was a sound of iron tools being moved around inside the sack. The man who was sitting stretched his hand out and the other man gave him something.

It was an iron rod shaped like an arrow.

The man sitting next to the animal pierced its neck with the pointed end. Paridhi felt her heart jump again. She could not fathom how the same man who had been caressing the dead animal a few minutes ago could now impale it from the neck to the mouth with the iron needle.

She hated it all. Leaving Juroni's side, she started walking home. Halfway through the winding lane, she heard Juroni's voice. She was running to catch up with her.

"Who are these people? Where have they come from?" she asked frantically.

"They are nomads, homeless people. I don't know where they have come from," Juroni replied.

"Why did they kill the Johamal? What will they do with it?"

"To eat it, of course! What else!"

"What? Do people eat Johamal?'

"Yes. These people do. I gather they will roast it; I've

heard people discussing it. These people also kill and eat Bonbonda, the wild male cat, and pangolins."

Paridhi did not ask any more questions. The word 'homeless' troubled her.

Afterwards too, these people were seen in the jungles and fields around their village. She heard that they went around sniffing for the places the Johamal inhabited. When the animal went on a hunt it gave out a scent to warn fellow hunters to leave it alone. Yet, sometimes the hunter became the hunted. The nomads roasted the catch in the field behind their village. They also collected the scaly skin of the pangolins. Nobody knew where these people came from every year. Blessed with the fertile landscape and their own paddy fields, the people did not mind the intrusion. These people appeared suddenly one day, and then disappeared as abruptly.

Paridhi often wondered about their way of life. They did not have a roof over their heads, they were never sure where their next meal would be coming from, yet that was the norm as far as their lives were concerned. Were they better off—roaming around in lands of their choice because they had nothing to lose—than those who, despite having roofs over their heads and the surety of food and clothes, still felt insecure?

Paridhi was not sure why her sudden wish to run away intertwined itself with the image of those nomads. She longed to know if other people felt the same way at some point in life, when an inner voice nudged them to set forth on an unknown journey and roam around, directionless.

Paridhi imagined a paint brush moving in lines on its own, piling colours onto a canvas. At some places the colours were laid thick, at others they had a lighter touch. Some corners were in shadows, while others were more prominent. From the labyrinth of colours, the contours of a face surfaced.

Whose face was it?

Was it Anuja khuri?

Yes, it looked like her. With a complexion like milk mixed with vermillion, it could only be Anuja khuri's. Her voice faded away slowly as she seemed to say—I wish I could go away somewhere-far, far away.

At times, Juroni came up with random strange information. Perhaps they were not unfamiliar to the adults, but for adolescents like them, they were.

"Hey, do you know about this?"

"What?"

"Can you believe, I heard that Prasanta khura goes to sleep with Urvashi pehi at night."

Right then, the person they called Kon-dada, who worked at Prasanta uncle's household, reached that spot. Dressed in khaki shorts and a short-sleeved shirt, the stocky man was on his way to the other side of the field to fetch their cows which were grazing there. With her index finger on her lips, Paridhi signaled to Juroni to keep quiet. As soon as he crossed the lane near the railway track, Juroni started again, "It's true! I have heard with my own ears when Junu borma was discussing it with my mother. When I enquired what they were talking about they shooed me off, but I heard anyway. I really feel bad for Anuja khuri."

"I get angry too. Why is she still living here? Why doesn't she go away to her parents' place?"

Paridhi was livid. She admired Anuja khuri. The woman was not only beautiful to look at, but she was also beautiful at heart too. She was very fond of Paridhi. And more than that, she introduced her to a world beyond—the beautiful, ethereal world of books. She would be ever grateful for being handed the key to a door which led to the source of nectar. Had she not been privy to that wonderful world she would perhaps not had had the mental urge to pick up the pen.

She felt sorry for the woman. That night as she went to bed thinking about what Juroni had said, she asked her mother, "Why doesn't Anuja khuri go back to her parents' place?"

Her mother sighed and said, "It isn't easy to go away like this. Once you are married…"

Paridhi did not let her finish and blurted, "Are all women like you?"

In response her mother only looked at her, her eyes widening.

"You don't have to gossip about others. Now go to

sleep," her mother reprimanded her and left her side. She was running away from her daughter. She knew what Paridhi was trying to tell her. Though Paridhi looked frail, from time to time an uncompromising individual seemed to surface from deep down. At night when her father, dead drunk and mumbling invectives, entered the house and her mother held onto him acting as a crutch so that he would not fall, Paridhi became extremely angry. Sometimes she made a strange proposal to her mother, "Let's the three of us take the train and go away somewhere."

She wanted to teach a lesson to her father.

But at this suggestion, her mother became quite angry and warned her, "Never utter these words again, I warn you! Today is the last."

Paridhi could not sleep, though. Wide awake, she wondered if all women were like her mother—accepting everything unquestioningly. From where did mothers gather such patience? How could they, fuming and blaming their own fate during the day, become cool like a river at night to bring restful sleep to thousands of tired eyes?

Anuja khuri's big red phot on her smooth forehead shone, announcing her marital status. When Prasanta, who worked in the irrigation department, got married, the villagers were taken aback. It became a hot topic. They whispered among themselves because they assumed that he would settle down with Urvashi.

Urvashi was the daughter of Babulal, a porter at the railway station. They used to live in a small cottage, a little away from the cluster of houses for other employees.

People did not remember from when Prasanta started visiting that cottage. Sure, from time to time, Urvashi used to help with household chores at Prasanta's house but when she became almost a part of the family people weren't exactly sure. Prasanta's mother was rather happy with the convenience of having an extra pair of hands to help with household chores after marrying off her two daughters, Mala and Malobika.

When Paridhi thought about Urvashi, whose family was from Bihar, an image of a wheat-complexioned girl, with eyes like two pools of water and breasts more pointed than usual, came up. Perhaps the young and virile Prasanta wanted to take a dip in the pool of that lush body.

Secrets always have a way of slipping through the cracks. That is why things which should remain within the walls of a house still escape to reach eager ears. So the couple's rendezvous did not remain confined to themselves; the news of their secret liaison soon spilled out into the public domain. The salacious gossip gathered momentum until it spread like wildfire.

Certain people were happier to talk about the affair than others. They were always on the lookout for something to criticise. Surely, they were not capable of appreciating tender feelings like the love of a man for a woman. Love. What was it? At the cusp of adolescence and youth, Paridhi was puzzled by the shrill words, the impatience and comments of the people, when it was to do with love between a man and a woman.

On the way back from school, as Paridhi and Juroni walked through the field, they often saw a pair of lovers sitting together. They tried to keep themselves hidden from prying eyes by sitting behind the half-burnt wall of the sugar mill. It was a place around which many myths had been built up. The pair holding hands looked like two shadows. Paridhi pretended not to see them. Later, she heard that when they were absorbed in talking to each other, a few youths from the village dragged the boy from there and beat him up severely. Yet, no one who was related to them was offended. Their excuse was that the pair had brought a bad name to the village.

Paridhi, on the other hand, thought that the words of love that the two shared let loose a flight of butterflies in myriad colours in that surrounding which was now derelict and devoid of human presence. Their intimacy, born out of wanting to be together, created a thing of beauty in a place so dead and derelict, and once they left the place, the green grass held on to the drops of colour falling off from the wings of the butterflies. Maybe they transformed themselves into the gorukhis, the wild, red cow berries that grow abundantly in muck, to brighten the patches of the green grass. Soon, the abandoned place became silent again.

Paridhi was unusually curious about the sugar mill. Whenever she found an opportunity, she asked her uncle about it. But he became evasive when she asked.

The area around Paridhi's village was conducive to

sugarcane cultivation. A Bengali man from Sonitpur had set up a mill there. The sugar mill was to the west of Paridhi's house, on the other side of the railway track. It was something the villagers had never seen before and so they made a beeline to inspect it as if it was a zoo. Even Paridhi's mother and her friends went. But after making a round there, Paridhi's borma decided to stop, adding sugar to her tea. She said whenever she saw the sugar granules, she could only picture the dirty feet of the labourers who were involved in the work of squeezing out the juice from the sugarcanes. However, many among the villagers worked there. They were happy that there was now a source of livelihood. But one day suddenly shouts ranted the air:

"Fire... fire... fire!"

People flew helter skelter. The sugar mill was engulfed in orange flames. They looked like devils dancing in an orgy as they lifted their hands skywards. The heat singed the hearts of the people who worked there. The building continued to burn for a few days.

Who were the arsonists? Whose envy or conspiracy did the mill give in to? Was it because the successful businessman was a non-Assamese or was it due to someone's hunger for the fertile land? Following the incident, policemen in khaki uniforms visited the site for a few days; they questioned a few people. Nobody knew what had really happened. They were simple people and yet to be exposed to the shenanigans going on beyond the village. Some of the labourers who had come to work at the mill took up tilling the field, some started making cane baskets, fans, etc. And the half-burnt wall stood forlornly as if to remind people 'There was once a sugar mill here'. By the time Paridhi's generation reached adolescence, it looked ghostly from a distance, covered in a thick layer of moss. The huge iron gate leading to the mill was a skeleton of its former self and was entrapped by wild creepers. It looked as if at a twist of a hand, the iron gate would break into myriad particles, like dry leaves crushed between two palms.

Without being conscious of it, Paridhi shook her hands as if to get rid of the dry, rough iron particles sticking to her palms. A nameless feeling overtook her; she felt her body tremble as if struck by a gust of cold wind. She shook her head a little to calm herself. She tried to shake off memories of the story of the water princess who was thirsty even while living in the water, living characters like the nomads, Urvashi and the young pair who looked for love amidst the defunct sugar mill.

8

"Hei Juroni! Why are you working this late? Don't you feel sleepy? Yesterday I heard the sound of your sewing machine going on almost till midnight." Paridhi rebuked her friend as soon as she stepped onto the mud-swept floor of her house.

"And you? What were you doing so late? Burying your head in the pages of a book, right? Who asked you to miss your sleep for that?" Juroni retaliated good-naturedly.

"What can I do? It's my passion. These days I don't find much time to read during the day."

"As for me, stitching clothes is a passion and profession both."

"Even then, don't over-stress yourself. Your neck will feel the pain over time."

"Oh, don't even talk about pain. My neck, back, waist, legs—all are victims of it. But what can I do? Without working how will I manage to buy household provisions and clothes? I am not fortunate like you. You don't have to worry about survival."

"Life is the same for all, you know. You think I am living a very comfortable life. Working constantly on the computer has made my bad eyesight worse. Now without glasses I can't see things even at a short distance," Paridhi replied as she used her forefinger to lift the glasses from the bridge of her nose.

Juroni sighed audibly and read out a long list of people who seemed to enjoy a good life. And then she abused the unseen god to her heart's content. Paridhi knew that the very next moment Juroni would beg her god mentally to forgive her. She smiled. Both of them engaged in hot debates when Paridhi found her friend visiting an astrologer who would apparently foretell her future; when she buried a talisman in the courtyard praying that her brother's temper would cool down even though she didn't particularly like him; when she organised a kirtan session by devotees to pray to the Lord when somebody in the family fell sick. She could not convince Juroni that all these had no meaning. Instead she had to face her friend's admonition, "You don't believe in anything, it's not good."

For some time after such a confrontation, Juroni would even refuse to speak to her.

However, the period of non-communication lasted only a few days. She could not stay away from Juroni. Somehow, despite holding different views, she found her closest to her heart.

"I had finished stitching your clothes quite some time back. I didn't have time to deliver them," Juroni said.

She took it out from a polythene bag. Paridhi inspected it. A set of white mekhela sador speckled with blood-red roses. Bondeep had presented the set to her quite some time back. He confided that he went around the bazaar to find exactly what he had wanted. He knew that she loved the combination of red and white. His eyes lit up with admiration when he saw her wearing dresses in this blend. Sometimes when she wore a churidar kameez set like this he even teased her, "Are you going to eat me up?" But these days he did not compliment her the same way. Did he even notice what she was wearing? She felt a resentment brewing in her mind sometimes but that did not mean she stopped wearing clothes in red. That day when she saw this pair of mekhela-sador, like a garden of roses, she felt her heart swell again with love for him. The fragrance of roses assailed her nostrils.

"What are you thinking of? Dying to wear this, right? Wear it and take a photograph and send it to your husband," Juroni teased her.

Juroni talked like this. She knew everything about her. How could Paridhi not divulge her thoughts about the person dearest to her heart? In the evening, when Juroni returned from the shop and did not have much pending work, she visited Paridhi's house without fail. As Paridhi did too, when she was free. When they were together, they visited their early years as schoolgirls. A courtyard of memories welcomed them with open arms. There, their dreams, their aspirations spread wings as moonlight washed over them.

Sure, as they grew up, their intellectual worlds, attitudes even, differed somewhat. But Paridhi felt close to this happy-go-lucky girl who loved people. Juroni did not throw out the left-over patches of clothes after an apparel was stitched. Instead, she turned them into dresses for the half-clad little children running around in their village. Their parents could not afford dresses for them. The little children's sunken eyes lit up with happiness when they saw the colourful dresses Juroni gave them. Perhaps those smiles acted like many-hued pollens of flowers to brighten Juroni's soul. Paridhi felt happy too for her friend's sake.

Juroni had appeared for the matriculation exam the same year as Paridhi. But she was not successful. She did pass the school final next year too and that was the end of her association with books and exams. Like Paridhi, life was leading her through a rough track of ups and downs. Her father, a farmer, had to manage a household of four daughters and a son.

Even when Juroni talked to her, the sewing machine went on non-stop. Paridhi's eyes slid down from Juroni's face and settled on the machine's wheel. Juroni's life seemed to mimic the relentless turning of that wheel.

After a lot of requests—begging even—and endless rounds in offices, Juroni had managed to receive the machine under a government scheme for self-employment for women. Within a short time Juroni became an expert seamstress. She was a hard-working farmer's daughter after all. At first, she took orders for small items, working mostly from home, but soon she bought another machine with her savings and opened a stall at the chariali, the junction.

As Juroni's income increased, her desire for a good life took off too. With layers of make-up and new dresses, Juroni now acquired a personality of her own—effervescent, always full of life and loquacious. That's why when 'Juroni Tailoring Shop' did not open its shutters sometimes, the chariali looked bereft of company. Her customers were not mere customers. They, as well as other shopkeepers in the vicinity, had become her friends. They shared their woes and happiness with her without any reservation. Juroni had this capacity of opening up the locks in people's minds and entering their private worlds.

"Now tell me about your very own person," Paridhi teased.

"Oh, who cares! I am least bothered. A nincompoop, that's what he is. He asks his mother's permission before doing anything. If he can't be by my side when I am in trouble, if he doesn't touch my head with understanding when I am suffering and cannot wipe tears from my cheeks, what's the use of my clinging to him? In fact, I don't seek him out these days. Sometimes if I suggest, let's go somewhere to sit quietly and talk, he gets worried that somebody will see us together and carry the story to his mother. Well, we are not in an age now to tremble in fear of parents for our love interest...what do you say? Fool!"

Juroni took a long breath after the tirade.

"If he is a man, he should be strong both physically and

mentally. He looks like a wrestler outwardly but inside he is weak. How can I think of starting a life together with a man like him? I need a man like the hero of a Hindi film; if needed he can punch someone who confronts him."

At one time seeing her father's uncouth behaviour, Paridhi's dreams of a special person of one's own had taken a back-foot, but then slowly, in adolescence, it hummed back to life somewhere in her inner world. She admired Aamir Khan no end. Today, she could smile remembering the girl when she was too young to judge his acting prowess or the aura of his personality and fell in love with him unconditionally. She used to scan the entertainment page of the newspaper her uncle subscribed to, checking to see whether there was any article or news about the star. She hunted for a pair of scissors as soon as she saw his picture in the newspaper. When she read romantic stories, she found in the hero an image of Aamir Khan.

People's dreams change with time. The faces in dreams get replaced by others. For Paridhi, the new face in her imagination was somewhat hazy. Perhaps she was waiting to discover that face.

Did Bondeep fit that image she had imagined?

Yes, he did. He surely did. But sometimes when she felt neglected and missed his attention, the teenage girl inside her shouted—no, no, it doesn't match.

"Even the strongest woman perhaps seeks someone on whose wide shoulders she can rest her head. Yes, you need a man as your own to live, but it's better to live alone than with a spineless one," Juroni asserted and then named a few single women she knew.

"Aren't they on their own? When I see them, it seems to me they are better off. They can do whatever they want, they can go wherever they want; they don't have to take anybody's permission for that. They are independent. In fact, it's men who can't live without us. You can see a lot of unmarried women, but how many men have you seen remaining bachelors?"

As she listened to Juroni, Paridhi's eyes strayed involuntarily to a huge trunk placed on a wooden stool in the corner of the room. She had seen on many occasions what was inside that box. Sets of mekhela-sador, a bedcover big enough for a double-bed, pillowcases with embroidery, handkerchiefs. She knew there were also a lightweight set of two bangles and a jewellery set designed in local Assamese style.

Did these indicate a desire to stay single? When someone really wants something, often on the surface they display a sense of nonchalance with words like, 'It doesn't matter, who cares.' She could sense that her friend was very unhappy. People only saw the vivacious girl dressed in bright hues but could they guess who the girl behind that façade was? Juroni to them was this strong, confident girl. But could they spot the soft and sentimental girl that lived inside her?

Half of Juroni's income was spent on maintaining her household. So she took it for granted that she had some special privileges. If she didn't get them, the head beneath the silky, shampooed hair flared up. After a day spent working hard, when Juroni returned home and had to make her own cup of tea to freshen up, her face clouded over, the colour of her cheeks faded. Her lips, coated in lipstick, rebelled and hard words against the people of the house spewed out from them.

Too arrogant, that's what the trouble is with her, her elder sisters complained.

People in her family saw her as arrogant. They did not see her yearning for love. Paridhi knew all this. She was her best friend after all.

Now they chatted about many things. In between, Juroni's elder sister brought a cup of tea with two biscuits for her. In their family of many girls, only the third was married. The eldest one's age was now on the wrong side of eligibility; the one after her was waiting... And here was Juroni, the youngest...waiting too, but going on with her work anyway. She had also taken agency from a well-known foreign cosmetics company. She knew how to communicate with people. She knew how to sell dreams to the young women who wanted to become beautiful with the help of the beauty products. Even Paridhi had to give in sometimes to her coaxing but in her case, Juroni did not take a commission.

"Let me go now. You have a lot on your hands."

Paridhi left, the rose garden ensconced in a polythene bag. The monotonous ghorr...ghorr...ghorr sound of the sewing machine followed her.

9

Paridhi and her mother had been extra-busy in the kitchen this morning. They cooked different kinds of curries and fries. Dipak and his family were going to arrive by lunchtime. Paridhi went early to the weekly Saturday haat to buy vegetables, meat and fish. Her mother had picked up various kinds of greens from the kitchen garden a day ahead. The air in the kitchen was now thick with the aroma of fish curry cooked with a generous amount of onion, tomato and carrots, a chicken curry, various kinds of fried greens, pointed gourd and brinjal slices dipped in a gram flour and water mix and fried golden brown, savoury fried balls with bhedailata creeper leaves, etc. The family was visiting after a long time. Her bordeuta must be also happy at his son's impending visit though he did not show it. Paridhi gave him an early bath and dressed him in fresh clothes. As he sat in the front verandah, he called out to Paridhi. She ran to attend to him though she was very busy. He was quite impatient these days, it was no use trying to make him understand.

Now at every few minutes' intervals, he asked: "Are they arriving before lunch?"

"Yes, bor-ta, they will."

"Why don't you call to find out where exactly they are now?"

"I did a few minutes ago. They were at Jorabaat."

"Oh, that's so? There's so much traffic these days, and most of the cars drive at high speed."

Paridhi slipped away quietly. Frankly, she neither had the time to attend to her uncle's anxious query, nor the inclination at the moment. She knew her uncle would now open the newspaper and worry aloud when reading about some road accident. She got irritated sometimes, but felt sad too, watching him in this state. These days he was often apprehensive. If one of them stepped out of the house, until their return he would remain restless. At such times, the one who remained at home would have to respond to his incessant queries. If a glass of water was kept near the edge of the table, he would become agitated and obsessed that it would crash to the floor. Until it was placed in the middle of the table, he could not be calmed down. In the evening he would ask umpteen times if the locks of the doors were fixed properly. At night too he slept in fits and starts. He complained that when he slept he had bad dreams. He found some men chasing him with spears and choppers and could not escape the attack. In short, he worried all the time and was also constantly agitated in the bargain.

Paridhi could understand why her uncle behaved like

this. He had crossed many hazardous canals in his life. Problems chased him one after another. Of course, who in this world has ever successfully evaded problems anyway? Life is an ocean of problems. But, unfortunately, the peace and relief her uncle deserved in his old age eluded him. His favourite son had taken a different path and then his wife died young. Both events affected him terribly. His elder son, Dipak, could bring him some solace but it was not to be. Demands of a job and livelihood made him choose the city where he had settled down with his family. Now Paridhi and her mother were the only ones who were by his side.

Sometimes Paridhi got depressed living alone in the company of two old, helpless people utterly dependent on her. She felt abandoned in the old house, its teakwood posts now home to termites. Often, she stared for a long time at the ceiling from where chunks of earth fell off. Would the rest fall off too, not as chunks but crumbling into particles, cascading down without a pause—little raindrops of soil, not water, on Paridhi as she stood below with her arms outstretched? The earth would cover her slowly and step by step her bones, her flesh would crumble and mix with the earth. That would bring to an end a chapter of sorrow that was set off by an understanding of the inevitable truth of life. Sometimes Paridhi was surprised at her imagination, foreseeing her own end like this.

But now, her thoughts returned to her uncle.

For eighty-two years, his life was entwined with this

world. Now, thinking of leaving it depressed him. He seemed convinced that he would not live for long. A few days ago, Paridhi had taken out the Srimadvatgita for him to read. There was a time when he used to recite from the scripture to find solace in troubled times. Perhaps he would find some peace in its pages, she thought. But she was disappointed. After perfunctorily going through some passages, he kept the book aside. One day, with Bondeep's help, she even took him to meet a psychiatrist. The doctor spent a long time talking with him alone. His verdict: because of advanced age, the neurons were drying up. He prescribed some medicines but also said that there was no hope of a complete cure. With time, his restlessness and depression would get worse. However, they could try their best to keep him out of mental stress. After being on medication for some time, she took him to the doctor again. At first, her uncle refused to go, declaring that he was not suffering from any illness. Bondeep needed his best persuasive power to make him agree to go. Her uncle trusted Bondeep. Paridhi had told him about her relationship with him. Afterwards, he asked Paridhi only one thing, "He is a Brahmin. Will his household accept you as a daughter-in-law?"

"Even if they don't, it doesn't matter. We are wedded mentally." She thought like this but kept silent in front of her uncle. Her mother looked at her too. She also expressed the same apprehension. Paridhi knew that her mother was not happy about her liaison with Bondeep. She was worried, naturally. But Paridhi was convinced that with time her mother was going to accept it.

In this clear sky of happiness, the only person who introduced a dark cloud was her cousin Dipak, her Shontu-da.

She recalled a time when he was still at home, yet to get a job. He had thrown a fit when he came to know about the relationship between his cousin and Bondeep.

Paridhi had just tasted freedom after her father's death but now another hard fist was trying to push her down again. True, Dipak was not an alcoholic like her father, but he too was bloated with the inherent ego of a man. He, like many men, regarded it his right to oppose a woman if she wanted to assert herself. He tried to smother the dream Paridhi at last dared to indulge in.

This was the same Dipak for whom she was cooking a chicken curry with sesame seeds now. It's difficult to understand how time changes many things. Human relationships are interlaced and complex, Paridhi admitted to herself. Sometimes they have to be maintained, even if mechanically, often against one's will, for the sake of the bloodline.

Paridhi covered the wok and decided to check on her uncle. She looked at her mother who was making a paste of mint leaves on the grinding stone in a corner. She gave her mother the steel bowl full of ground ginger and garlic before leaving the kitchen.

As she stepped onto the verandah, she found that her uncle was not there. Her heart skipped a beat. Where was he? His head would spin even if he took a few steps. Had he fallen down somewhere? She ran through the passage to the main gate of the house and looked up and down. She saw him now on the other side of the road, craning his neck to look in the distance and checking his wristwatch. Paridhi walked up to him quickly. Scolding him for stepping out on his own, she held his hand and led him back home. She made him sit on a chair in the verandah and went to lock the gate outside. Joydev was passing with unsteady steps. She tried to escape, pretending not to see him, but failed.

"How are you, Pari?" he asked, the words slurred.

Paridhi answered with a perfunctory 'I am fine' and looked at him. His wasted frame seemed ready to buckle down at any moment. His once-athletic body had shrunk long back. This is what alcohol does, Paridhi thought to herself. He was mumbling something, but she did not comprehend what he was saying. She looked at his eyes. They were bright red, bloodshot. The bulging eyes seemed ready to jump out from the sunken holes. These were the kind of eyes that kept Paridhi ensconced in fear for many years of her young life.

"Life is very strange, do you understand Pari? You hanker for something and until you get it you are restless, but once you get it you lose the taste for it. Now the taste of happiness is there only in one thing... see here!" Joydev mumbled and fished out a white polythene packet from the pocket of his loose pants and declared loudly, "Real taste of life!" The packet contained a liquid—it looked familiar, like the opaque water you get after you wash rice grains in it. It was sulai, country liquor—the real taste of life for Joydev.

"Real taste of life," he repeated a few times. Paridhi excused herself saying there was work to be finished in the kitchen. She wondered what object from the house Joydev had sold today to enjoy his taste of life.

These days, his mother tried her best to hide things from Joydev. She gave him twenty rupees every day to buy his drink from the money she earned by selling milk. If she didn't, she faced trouble. His vulgar abuses even reached the walls of the neighbour's house. But often the twenty rupees was not enough for Joydev. He often picked up some or the other household item to sell. The things he had bought once with his earnings dwindled in number—the kanh, or bell-metal plates, the bowls, the baanbati, or the bowls with stands, glasses, water-jugs, cups and saucers—you name it. Much before that had disappeared the TV set, home theatre, mobile phone, pressure cooker, hot-case for keeping food warm, flask, even bulbs. When the house had only one kanh dish left for serving food, his mother ate from a plantain leaf while she served him on the dish. One day he took even that to the bhati-khana. When his mother could not find it, she understood what had happened. In anger she served him rice on the kitchen floor itself. And he ate like that without objecting too! Then Joydev's eyes fell on the soft blanket she had carefully kept packed. Once upon a time, he himself had bought it for her. Even if she shivered in the wintry nights, she kept it aside like a treasure and had not used it yet. From time to time, she took out the blanket from the box, ran her fingers over its silky surface and then packed it again to store it away. When she did not find it in the box one day, she cried so much sitting on the courtyard, thumping her chest, that people thought Joydev had died.

One day he asked for the light gold chain that he had once bought for her. When she refused, he dragged her by her hair. Some men in the neighbourhood got incensed at this and dragged him to a betel-nut tree, bound him by a rope and were ready to beat him with a cane stick. But his mother stopped them, begging, "Please don't beat my son!" The men left, disgusted. That night Joydev threw a chair at the looking glass attached to the Godrej almirah. His mother cut her fingers while picking up the shards.

Thus, the house once full of luxuries was left with nothing now, not even a chair to sit on.

The stature Joydev had enjoyed in society had long disappeared, like the flesh on his body. Additionally, he became a topic of gossip and mockery by the villagers in their leisure time. Once, when he had visited a cousin, she had sent a big packet of sticky rice, bora-chaul, but it never reached his home—it went straight to the bhati-khana. The almirah where his mother had kept pairs of mekhela-sador was almost empty. Once, his maternal aunt came visiting and brought a new sador as a present for his mother. It disappeared by the time she reached home. Now the pillow-covers were also gone. If he did not find a bag to carry rice or lentil, stolen from the larder, he slipped off the pillow-covers to carry his stolen wares. Once he finished with the big items, he started on the smaller ones. Face-cream his mother used, coconut oil bottles, packets of detergent powder, biscuit packets, etc. Even a two-rupee sachet of shampoo did not escape his eagle eyes. People were surprised—how much liquor could he get in exchange of these small items? But Joydev was clever. To the shampoo sachet he would add some tea leaves, a few dry chillies, half a tube of toothpaste and so on till the selling price came up to ten or twenty rupees—enough to get a few gulps. Even the vegetables disappeared from time to time. His mother tried to find new places to hide them, but he soon found out. At times she even hid potatoes and tomatoes in the folds of a quilt. She kept the tin containing rice in the neighbour's house and when he left for the bhati-khana, she went to bring just enough rice for a meal. She filled polythene packets with lentil, flattened and hid them at the bottom of the almirah with the broken glass. Even that place was soon discovered. Then his mother tied a rope to the packet, fixed it on the clotheshorse and on top of it, kept her folded clothes. She prayed to the Lord to forgive her for keeping food underneath the clothes she wore, a sacrilege. But people laughed uproariously, talking about how things which are supposed to be in the kitchen found new homes in Joydev's house.

Paridhi smiled sometimes too but was also surprised. She had never heard of or seen anyone stripping a house to the bone to satisfy the thirst for drinks.

She shook off these thoughts that depressed her,

switched off the gas burner and took off the wok with the chicken curry. She heard the horn of a car in the courtyard. Her uncle called out to her. "Have they arrived?" Both mother and daughter ran to receive the guests.

10

The quiet house with only three people was now full of sound. The grandson's half-pronounced words and unsteady walk made Paridhi's uncle ecstatic. He perhaps also felt assured that there was now someone to carry on his bloodline; a half-dead tree trunk now showed off a new shoot. Though his body refused to comply, he forced himself to pick up the baby and make him sit on his lap and caressed his head. The baby, on the other hand, like a bird with new wings, did not want to keep sitting and wanted to explore the open courtyard. He muttered to himself in his own language and clapped his hands with palms soft like cottonwool. Watching him, her uncle's face lit up with an indescribable joy. The scene touched Paridhi too. As she looked at her beloved uncle, Paridhi thought wistfully—Ah! If happiness could brighten people's life like this always! She picked up the baby, like a rose in bloom, from the courtyard and took him inside to her room. She hid her nose in the soft brown hair covering his round head and took a long breath. That soft scent, typical of all babies, filled her mind with a great sense of peace. She took a selfie with the baby and posted it on Facebook. Seeing it, Bondeep teased her on the phone, "Hey! You look like a mother!"

"Oh, how you go on!"

"One day won't you yearn for a live doll like him?"

"When you are there, who else do I want?" she said softly.

She knew Bondeep loved children. He could not stop himself from holding a baby close to his chest whenever he met one. Perhaps he nursed a dream of becoming a father with her as his wife.

There is no end to one's yearnings. People like to plan for posterity. Something to leave behind for the next generation to remember them by. But Paridhi dreamt of something else. One day, as she rested her head on Bondeep's shoulder, she blurted out, "Do you know what I want, Deep? I want to adopt an orphan girl. She'll be all mine."

Bondeep paused and then lifting her face with his palms looked into her eyes and asked, "I haven't been able to fulfill all your desires, isn't it?"

Paridhi kept quiet. Sometimes she questioned herself. She loved Bondeep deeply but even then, at times she felt like something was amiss. Was she like that water princess too? Submerged in water but still thirsty? Why did she feel like going away somewhere at times? Why did she feel an urge to give all her love to an orphan child? Despite having someone who loved her dearly? And honestly, she did dream of a life with him. Bondeep supported her in everything she did, but in this matter she was not that sure. Perhaps he thought this wish was a result of her over-sensitive mind. Paridhi understood that and she never ever brought up the subject again. But secretly she nursed the dream nonetheless, and when she found time to indulge in her thoughts, that dream recurred...maybe one day!

"Pari! Please come here!" It was Bithika, her sister-in-law, Shontu-da's wife. She excused herself from Bondeep's call, promising to revert later. She saw that the little bundle of joy was now examining the boxes on her dressing table. The face cream was on the floor. She picked it up. She kept the bottle of coconut oil out of his reach and left the baby with her mother as she went to the backyard.

Dipak's wife was not used to handling the tube well. So Paridhi filled two buckets of water and carried them to the bathroom. Bithika was brought up in a house where she never lacked any comfort. Her father owned quite a few good guest houses in the city. Working as an officer in an insurance company, Dipak also tried his best to see to it that she did not lack any comfort. Bithika faced a few problems when she visited her in-laws' house in the village. There was no western-style toilet, no tap water, no shower in the bathroom, no Dunlop mattresses, and most of all—here she had to wear mekhela-sador all the time, at her father-in-law's house. Oh, if she had to live here and look after her father-in-law and family, what a state she would have been in, Paridhi thought sometimes and smiled. Her aunt died young due to complications of diabetes. Had she and her mother not been here, who would have looked after her uncle? Whenever she felt like going away somewhere, her uncle's face drew her back. And then there was her mother.

People are bound by ties they cannot deny.

Yet sometimes, they distance themselves from one another. They refuse to stick to each other, wanting something else. There is no end to what one wants.

Wants, wants, wants. Like a never-ending folktale, the desire for more goes on and on. Sure, desire for a better life is a part of human aspiration. But how much is too much? The thought crossed Paridhi's mind often.

The government was building a four-lane highway skirting their village. So many people had to give up some land in the forecourt. Of course, they received compensation for the land given up and the trees that had to be cut. Even houses had to be demolished. In such cases, they received extra money. Paridhi was astonished when she found out that the teacher she had respected from her childhood, like many others, had bribed the engineer who was in charge of measuring the land to calculate the adequate compensation to jack up his area so that he could claim more money. That engineer was once his student.

Was she stupid to expect better from a society bowing

to the god of consumerism? If without much labour extra money came in, what was the harm? She knew that not a single member of the village panchayat did anything for anyone without some kind of bribe. Under government schemes for the poor arrived material for repairing houses after floods and storms as also blankets, mosquito nets, water filters, etc. Those who suffered the losses remained in the same state, still living under roofs with holes and trembling in winter, bitten by mosquitoes. Those who already had houses of their own built more houses. Nobody knew in whose almirah the mosquito nets and the blankets were safely stored away.

Observe the grotesque dance of money!

Was that all? Paridhi had witnessed so many incidents, like two neighbours bickering over the boundary line between two houses which sometimes led to physical fights.

Boundaries. Yes, boundaries that spoil relationships.

When she thought of the word, her mind brought her to her childhood. When she was in primary school, Paridhi hated drawing maps in geography class. To her then, those staggered lines did not hold any meaning. She used to get annoyed that she could not draw the lines at her will. They were already demarcated—she could only follow them. Lines that went awry had to be rubbed off with an eraser.

How can restless childhood stick to rigid lines? Used to the freedom of roaming at will, how could she enjoy drawing a land encircled with already-set lines? Instead, she loved to draw the sun, moon, stars, birds and the river. They could never be bound by man. Only for the sake of getting marks in the exam she practiced drawing the maps: the red part of the pencil drew the borders and the blue one to indicate the river and the hills. At first it was the map of the district, then the state of Assam and next, extending to the map of India. Maybe that's how one's birthplace extends its own border—from the district to the state... then to the country and then to other continents...

Not really. In school they never had to draw maps of the world. But for her it was the easiest thing. You just draw a big circle and done! If you added two ears, two eyes, a nose and a mouth and some hair on top, look, it became a man's face. So easy! Once, Paridhi read somewhere about a little boy whose father gave him some scraps of paper and said that he had to join them together to find the hidden map of the world. The boy was puzzled. So many pieces of paper. How could he find the map of the world? But he did it, and perfectly too. On the other side of the paper his father had torn, there was a man's face. The boy sorted through the pieces and then joined them together, using the man's face as the guide. He found that the map of the world came up.

Though she did not like the idea, Paridhi tried her best to draw the map correctly. To make the border prominent, she moistened the pencil's red point with saliva and soon her tongue became red. At that age, she could never imagine that one day to mark a boundary, a highway could turn red with blood. Or, in that crimson tide, the map of human beings could get obliterated.

These days in her subconscious mind she often saw a litany of brown bodies. Like madmen they searched for something. When they failed, their sunken yellow eyes lit up like burning embers. The unusually white and sharp nails on their thin brown fingers sought out other bodies and scrapped at the flesh in a vicious attack. Drops of blood dripped to the earth. Pieces of flesh sullied the soil. And suddenly, the colour of the earth changed.

Why do the brown figures attack each other?

What do they want?

Paridhi scolded herself for letting her imagination stray like this. But often, nothing seemed to attract her—the kisses, dreams, sleep, food, the rhythm of life, songs. In such a state of mind, she wondered how people could continue to participate in the play of life as if nothing were amiss. Her eyes drooped, tired. She tried to catch a glimpse of something nebulous floating in the mist. The truth about life? Two unseen hands seemed to bring to her lips a cup full of bitterness. Her reflection in the mirror broke into a thousand pieces and she walked barefoot on the shards of glass.

It surprised her no end that people, capable of so much love, love that transported them to another plane, were also capable of shedding the blood of fellow men. They built walls around them to ensure safety, but were they really safe from each other?

For a simple, ordinary girl like Paridhi, these shades of life posed a puzzle that she was incapable of solving.

Dipak and his family left after two days. Before leaving, Dipak hinted at the urgent need to organise matters like disposal of the house, land, etc. now that his father was unwell. Perhaps he secretly worried that his father would give everything to Paridhi. She understood it pretty well, though nothing was said openly. She had long learnt to read people's minds, a lesson that life had taken care to teach her well. Her cousin and his father were made of two different metals. The idea of doing something for someone without expecting anything in return was foreign to Dipak.

But Rupak!

Her uncle's second son was the opposite of his elder brother. His heart was full of love for everybody. When he was a student in Guwahati, she heard from others that he picked up hungry children from the street and shared his food with them. He saved part of his pocket money to buy clothes for them though his nose was buried in books most of the time. His father dreamt of a bright future for his brilliant son. But the people in the family did not have an inkling about Rupak's own dreams. One day, the post-graduate student disappeared suddenly. Paridhi was quite young at that time. She heard words like *sangathan*, organisation, freedom, need for change and so on but could not understand much. She heard from others that Rupak went away dreaming of change. He loved the forest and now he made it his abode.

Meanwhile, his father lost the dream he had nurtured for long.

How fearful were those days!

At night, the villagers barricaded themselves at home in terror. Even the familiar train's whistle scared them. Their ears were always alert, ready to catch the sound of a knock on the door. What could they do? If they did not allow them to stay the night there was danger; if they let them in, there was danger then too. If they did not provide what they wanted there was a threat to life; if they did, there was threat from those who were searching for them. Even before the dawn broke, the doors opened. People did not know where they disappeared to in the blink of an eye. Gradually, the villagers stopped leading a normal life even during the day. The ground trembled under the trampling boots, and so also trembled the people inside the houses. Without any given reason, young men were picked up from houses. When they returned home many of them showed signs of physical torture. They heard some of them were even given electric shocks. On many nights, the jawans searched houses at random. If people somehow came to know about an imminent search operation, they asked the young men to leave home and hide in the forest. The young women were petrified of even moonbeams filtering through gaps in the reed walls. The villagers had heard about incidents in some places where the men in green, those who were there to ensure safety, raped girls and married women.

The families of those whose sons had joined the sangathan were particularly scared. On many occasions, Paridhi's house was the target of those gun-toting men in green. Her old uncle was hauled up from bed and questioned for hours. He was compelled to show the letters from Rupak. An Assamese member of the troop translated them into Hindi. One day, finding her drunken father in the room, the men beat him up mercilessly. For the next few days her father could not get up from the bed because of the pain. Even Dipak was picked up one day. He went through terrible physical torture. It took him long to recuperate.

For a group of people who went out seeking the sun for their own land, another innocent batch paid the price. Helplessly, Paridhi's uncle wrote to Rupak: "The sun you are looking for is only a mirage," but without any clue to an address the letter was only a token of a protest to be crushed in his tightened fist.

Nation and land—these two were at the centre of those boys' dream and they set out to the labyrinthine forest seeking a solution. The sun, with its warmth and promises of a better tomorrow, kept their hopes alive. Their decision of personal sacrifice and determination never to compromise made them go on. For their dream, they were ready to pay any price. When she grew up a little, Paridhi bowed with respect to that rising sun. She considered the boys heroes.

She was not alone. As they launched their movement—their idealism, the sacrifices they had made, the aim to uproot corruption that bogged Assamese society and bring about a change—were welcomed by the common people.

But somewhere something went wrong. Afterwards, the same people were compelled to declare they were killers, they were looters. They were not heroes, they were cowards.

Those boys who set off on the path of idealism now started targeting the common people. When they started out, they declared war on those who indulged in corruption, but now, their leaders indulged in the same pursuits. If someone opposed, they did not hesitate to aim the firearm they carried along always close to their chests. In the name of obtaining their own land, they let flow streams of blood of their own kinsmen. Even innocent children did not escape their guns and bombs. Who could support all this?

Paridhi's uncle wrote again: "In the name of ushering in a new sun of hope you have only brought darkness to the state. You are destroying yourselves, taking a decision fraught with inexperience and thoughtless sentiment. People are scared of moving around freely, they are afraid of talking freely. With promises of an elusive freedom, you have only jailed them. Remember, above everything, what matters is people. Whatever is the aim, where they become of secondary interest, where their tears and blood merge, people lose belief in the so-called sun. We don't want that kind of freedom in exchange of common man's blood. Let the darkness of night remain. You all come back. Come back."

When she thought of these words, tears filled up Paridhi's eyes. Rupak-da's bright face that she last saw in her childhood emerged from her memory. He used to write poetry. One day, her uncle had himself brought out an old notebook, its pages worn-out, from his ramshackle wooden almirah and handed it to her. She accepted it with deep reverence. Her heart wept as she read the poems full of respect and love for his own people, for his own land. She desperately wanted to ask Rupak-da: Did the metal instrument in your hand pierce somebody's chest? Did the gushing blood from the heart make your head spin? The person in you who loved people, didn't it accuse you of heartlessness? Did the person who thrashed about in the throes of death make the man on the other end die slowly? When you were the ones who supplied the bomb to the shadowy figures and the little children turned instantly into chunks of raw flesh...how could you still continue to live?

Was anything just easy?

The questions whirled round and round in her mind. In place of Rupak-da's face floated in Paras' face. In the struggle to free themselves from the shackles of central control, two young men of the same family had disappeared forever. Rupak went off on his own accord but their mistaken path compelled Paras to leave this world. Her dear brother, Paras, who wanted to live free of boundaries, like the wind.

11

When the evening mist
Will cover the field of rush
And the wild ducks
Will whisper about the coming winter
I will think of you, my dear

Mayur had sent the message. A soft smile flit across Paridhi's lips as she read it. Mayur was writing to her after a long time. He was a man of the forest. He could be anywhere, anytime. And then suddenly like the rare blue moon, he made an appearance.

"Have you written it? But which of the butterflies have you dedicated it to?" Paridhi teased him.

"No luck. Actually, a Japanese soldier posted at the border had written it. I don't know his name. I liked it and so am sending it to you."

"Ok, now update me about yourself. How far are you in your research?"

"It won't take long. I have almost finished. I promise I'll publish it with you and your partner. And you'll launch the book."

"No, no, I can't. Choose some well-known writer," Paridhi demurred.

"Okay, okay!" Mayur agreed but requested her to write an introduction that could go on the dust jacket.

He had many dreams about the book. It would be illustrated with photographs of the butterflies and so it had to be multi-coloured. Of course, it would increase the production cost. His father could not afford to bear the whole cost. His elder aunt was going to chip in too. Even then, he needed more funds. So he was searching for sources. Paridhi did not know much about his family. Mayur hardly talked about them. She came to know him through Facebook a year ago. He was familiar with her writings in different publications. While sending a friend request, he had also written comments on them and sent them through an SMS. That was the beginning of their friendship. They became close enough to address each other with the familiar toi. He was about three months younger to her.

Mayur said that he would see to it that his book was supplied to schools and colleges once it was published. With the money he got from its sale, he planned to finance education for needy children.

He liked to share all these dreams with Paridhi. She, however, did not know what his own dream was, apart from helping the poor.

After the chat, he sent her a picture of a butterfly with a message: "Look at this. A rare one."

"So pretty!" she replied, as she examined the insect, its white wings spotted with muga, yellow and black dots. But then which butterfly in the world is ugly? Its very body mirrors the beauty of creation.

"But its name is strange," he wrote.

"What?"

"Witch! But it's not an ogress."

"Oh, I understand, mohini, one that entices. In any case, you are already entrapped by the magic of butterflies."

"No, never! No living thing in the jungle entraps you. If you enter it with a pure heart the jungle enchants you, loves you. Rather, I find people more complicated. They cause much pain to others. But as soon as I enter the jungle all my troubles, pain, fall away. I feel refreshed."

Mayur really loved the jungle. He breathed with the leaves of the trees, he found the colour of life in the wings of the butterflies. The jungle was in his conscious life and in the subconscious mind too. It was his home, he found something unfathomably pleasurable in nature's company.

"You know, there's a reason why some people leave the regular life and respond to the call of the forest," Mayur had told her one day. "There's a certain serenity, a peace in its womb."

Should she ask him why he became a man of the forest? Was it only because of the call of nature, or something else? Then she abandoned the idea—let him be, she decided.

Sometimes she envied Mayur. She felt that only those who had the heart to appreciate the beauty of the wilderness tasted the real sweetness of life on earth.

Even she felt like responding to the loving call of nature at times. True, she couldn't set off to the forest at will, but she at least could invite the green of the valleys and trees to enter her inner self. Often in her imagination, she became a child again, walking barefoot on the lichen-covered grass. It was a land where there was no restriction, no unwelcome force trying to keep her back from her destination.

Paridhi has grown up now. Those days when she hid herself in a dark corner underneath the bed were gone. Even those days of dreaming of a hero in a Hindi film coming alive were long over. The days of tears trickling down, wetting her cheeks as she heard the story of the water princess seemed buried in memory now. Those who knew her, people around her, considered her a practical, mature girl. But when she was with Bondeep, sometimes she craved to put aside all her intellectual activities, her opinions on current political affairs and just become a little girl who walked barefoot on the expanse of his broad chest. A little girl who would happily draw pictures here and there, on earth, on sand; a little girl who did what she wanted to under the protective umbrella of the man she loved.

Perhaps man's suppressed desires wait for a chance to break free. After a difficult time during which one is forced to bear it all silently, times change for the better, and all the hidden wishes try to escape as if from behind a closed door.

There was a time when Paridhi hesitated even to pick up a fallen leaf wondering if deuta would become angry.

She remembered that day very well indeed.

Paridhi wanted to draw a blood-red sun and slightly moistened a piece of paper. Suddenly, she felt a strong hand pulling her hair resting at her nape. Then he dragged her to the courtyard, abusing her throughout. Paridhi was stunned. What had she done? A pain from the base of the neck climbed up to her head.

Her mother ran from the kitchen. She cried out, "Why are you doing this? What's she done? Please leave her."

Her father uttered words not fit for civilised ears and shouted, "I've asked her for a glass of water so many times. Did she get up? Oh, showing off as an artist, is she? Art art art at all times. I am a stupid man to live in this house, a fool. Y'all don't care for me. I've warned her so many times, this art, whatever it is, is not for this house. But no, she doesn't care. I am keeping a watch, I tell you. One day I'll cut you two, mother and daughter, to pieces, you'll see."

He pushed her with all his force and she crashed onto the rain-fed muddy courtyard.

"And you yourself—did you hear me calling you?" Now her father dashed towards her mother. She was trembling in fear. The man was shaking in rage. All the blood in his head seemed to gather in his face. It looked like a ball of fire. His wife's silence seemed to work like ghee in fire, stoking it. With all his force he pulled her mother's hair; her head turned left to right, right to left. The long black hair escaped the knot. It covered her back.

The moist paper where she wanted to draw a red sun took on the black of her mother's hair.

Ah, how those thoughts, memories, flowed from one to another! Like movie reels, the scenes rolled on. Her writings, studies, painting on pebbles, assisting Bondeep's publication house, taking care of her elderly uncle, helping her mother in the kitchen, having tiffs with Bondeep on the phone, keeping in touch with people she knew, keeping up with Facebook, WhatsApp messages. Even then she felt lost sometimes as though she was somewhere else too. Whenever an opportunity came, she stood at that time when teardrops and colour merged together.

One day, her father threw her water colour box into the well in the backyard. Paridhi agonised over it but could not understand why her father was so against her love for painting. Even then, was he able to stop her? The thing was, even if she wanted to stop, the colours pursued her. Sometimes she was in two minds about continuing with her hobby but the colours did not let her go.

Look at her now! She drew a window with pastel colours. Mixing black and blue, she made the interior of the house take on the shade of dark clouds. From the window emerged a long hand. She painted it in light yellow. The tips of the fingers were red.

"What are you drawing? Let me see."

Paridhi did not know that Paras had been standing behind her for a while, watching her. Shocked at his voice, Paridhi covered the picture with her hands. She did not want to show her drawings to anyone. Fearing that her father would find out, she kept them hidden at the bottom of her mother's old, rusted tin trunk. In the hole of the termite-ridden sal wood posts she stored the sticks of pastel colours.

She used the tong still in use to put coal in her aunt's old iron to retrieve the coloured chunks which looked like pieces of a candle. The old-style iron with a wooden handle, though a little rusted, was almost communal property in the neighbourhood. The tong was used to pick up a few firewood embers to put them inside the open mouth of the iron. Then it was fanned profusely before the cover was shut firmly. Her aunt would hold the wooden handle of the iron with a rag and then run it over her husband's dhoti-punjabi and her mekhela-sador spread on the floor.

Paridhi wanted to do it too, seeing how the clothes became wrinkle free. She wanted to run the iron on her mother's wrinkled clothes.

Paras pulled aside Paridhi's hands to see the painting.

"Oh, it's not nice, forget it," she said with a grumpy face.

"Why, it's quite good," Paras commented.

Paras looked again at the painting and then took it with him as he went out of the room.

"What are you doing? Wait!" Paridhi called as she ran after him and then like a car suddenly braking stopped at the doorway. An unknown young man was sitting on the bench in the verandah. The stranger was inspecting her painting with great concentration. Paridhi, now struck with shyness, shrunk into herself. She was a bit angry too at her elder brother's audacity. Why should he go around showing her work to strangers? Her restless mind persuaded her to paint, that's all. She muttered to herself unhappily and went inside. After some time, Paras came to tell her to make two cups of tea. Paridhi prayed that her father would not appear suddenly as she heated the water.

As the water boiled in the saucepan, she could hear the animated conversation between the two young boys. Was it discussion on her painting, she tried to eavesdrop but failed.

Paras somehow passed his higher secondary exam but after that, he abandoned any attempt to study further. He travelled with a theatre group from village to village, town to town. Perhaps he tried to find himself, his truth, his purpose through acting. At such instances, the young man seemed much more mature than his age. The first time he received the best-actor prize in a competition, he bought Paridhi a water-colour box, brushes from No 1 to 5 and two thick drawing pads.

Incidentally, the role he had enacted was that of a drunkard.

That particular day, Paridhi did not know why Paras asked her to accompany him to the railway station after lunch. Their relationship had everything a brother-sister duo should have as siblings—tenderness, requests for a favour, complaints, small frictions. But he had never asked her before to go along with him to the station as Juroni did. The siblings never thought of revealing to each other the layers of thought, light and dark, gathering secretly in their minds.

They were sitting under the sun at the platform. Sometime back, the train from Guwahati on its return journey had passed by. Though it disappeared from sight, the earth still shook with the impact of its speeding sound...*jhak... jhak...jhak*. Paridhi's mind too was trembling like the earth in the aftermath. It happened like this often. A departing train left behind a throbbing echo in her heart. For some moments, she felt disconnected with her surroundings.

"Now take this."

Paridhi woke up as if from a trance as Paras handed her something. Before the train arrived Paridhi had borrowed a fifty paisa coin from Paras and placed it on the railway track. Now Paras gave her the misshaped coin. She listened intently to what Paras was saying as she turned the coin in her palm again and again.

"Was I acting really that day? No. I only transformed myself into the man I have seen from my childhood. When people clapped, I found it hard to hold back my tears—the pain was too intense. You know Pari, I feel very lonely sometimes. But for you and Ma, I would have left this house long ago. Since I can remember, a particular smell has driven me mad. If I find any of my companions drinking, even for a day, I cut off that relationship. When I get a whiff of that smell all the blood in my body gathers in my head. You'll see Pari, I will demolish the bhati-khana in the village. I'll do it, you'll see."

Suddenly his voice took on a hardness she had not encountered before. Though she was young, Paridhi could empathise with the pent-up resentment and anger in her brother. She too suffered the same way. She instantly hated anyone she found drinking. She hated equally those who sold the liquid. What was the attraction, she wondered, as the putrid smell made her feel like throwing up. She too had to breathe in that horrid smell from a very young age. When sober, her father hardly said a few words, but he completely changed after a few gulps. Then he talked nineteen to the dozen. The thickened tongue pronounced words which made no sense. Those were words of resentment, complaints about others, and so on.

What drove him? What stoked him? Paridhi often wondered if this thing called sura made hidden pain boil over and with the first drop, made even a dumb man become garrulous.

Why do people drink? Young Paridhi had tried to find the answer everywhere, and often. It was not that people only drank to drown sadness. When there was surplus money from the donations for a raas-bhaona performance or Rongali Bihu in spring, they spent it on drinks and a dinner of rice with meat curry. Yes, even in pleasant situations people drank. Was it just an excuse? A crutch during times of sorrow, and elixir in times of bliss? When she saw her father losing his senses after a bout of drinking, Paridhi wanted to tell the seller at the bhati-khana, "Please, please listen, do you know by selling a bottle you are bringing darkness to a family's life?"

That day at the station platform, Paras confided in her many of his thoughts—his dilemmas, dreams, apprehensions. He wanted to make a children's film. He had thought about the plot too. He hoped that one day celluloid would give life to the story he kept alive in his heart. A few days ago, he had accompanied Kollol-dada to the Children's Film Festival in Guwahati and watched a film, a classic of sorts, and from then on, he had carried this dream close to his heart. Kollol-dada was a guru to Paras and others of his age. He himself wrote the scripts and gave them acting lessons. The boys listened to his advice with great attention. Paras had told him about the script he had written mentally. In reply, Kollol-dada had said, "Remember, for that you'd have to keep the child in you alive."

The Ahin sunlight was getting weaker now. The two siblings got up to leave. On the other side of the track, the green sheaves of the paddy, pregnant with the first seeds, fondly hugged the golden light of the evening.

Paridhi was now in class nine. She was not too bright a student, but her uncle had high hopes for her. He thought that even if she did not do exemplarily in the Matric exam, she at least would get a first division. Paridhi often felt like bowing down in gratitude to her uncle. If not for him, she would not have come this far. Growing up under his protective guardianship, she still yearned for a father who could be different from the one she had. When she thought of it, she choked with wistfulness. She often dreamt of a little girl unsteadily learning to walk. Her soft feet, like two newly sprung shoots, were about to lose balance and then a strong finger caught her in time. Whose finger should it have been?

Sometimes in her dream, Paridhi saw herself trying to walk to the main gate through the muddy courtyard. Somebody warned from behind, "Be careful! It's very slippery."

Should it not have been her father's voice?

Even in her dream, Paridhi became tired…walking…walking. But somebody gave her his shoulder to rest her head on. Should it not have been her father's?

She hankered for the reassuring voice of a father figure telling her, "Why are you worried my little Ma-joni? See, I am here!"

Perhaps people do not get all the things they want in life. Many dreams remain just that—dreams. By the time she was an adolescent, Paridhi had come to understand this. A tall girl with a slightly round figure and an attractive face dominated by a pair of big eyes that reflected the sad stories of harsh reality. This is how Paridhi looked now. She cried inwardly but did not allow herself to turn disillusioned. In her own way, she tried to turn those hard stories into something else with a poetic brush stroke. The more that hard times tried to snatch colour away from her, the more adamant she became about adding it back to her life.

There was a wooden box her mother had given her that had originally belonged to her great grandmother. Now it was filled with hundreds of red sandalwood seeds. In a plastic box she kept the seeds of bhatkhila tree, tokou palm, yellow nahar flowers and latumoni, the seeds of the creeper that goldsmiths used as weights. Many of them she found around her surroundings. She enjoyed collecting them. She painted on the hard seeds of the nahar and tokou trees and stored them in a glass jar. She dried pumpkin seeds and after painting them, glued them on a paper in the fashion of beautiful flowers. The latumoni seeds were so pretty—as if someone had tenderly painted them in two shades of red and black. When they emerged from under their dry sheaths, they filled her heart with instant happiness.

Paridhi was also very fond of the red sandalwood seeds. She looked on enchanted when sunlight brightened them even more. Some of her friends ate them too, but she could not. When she took them in her palms, the slippery seeds poured out like raindrops. She loved the sound of them sliding out of her palms. Ah, they looked like little hearts in orange mixed with red. Like red pearls, they retained their colour for a long time.

Nature, so rich with thousands of colours!

Nature, so generous with her treasure that it could bring a smile to the saddest face.

That's why Paridhi liked to explore the jungle on her

own sometimes. Nature also offered her courage to go on. Slowly she learnt to ignore the unreasonable demands of her father. She loved sitting beside the lane in the field behind her house and looking at the sky; to her, it looked like a blue sheet of paper where the sun sketched the lesson of life. She ached to become the bird on the top of the bamboo-and-straw scarecrow placed in the paddy field.

She liked to stand in the shade of the Simolu tree, on the other side of the railway station. For many years, the tree stood there with great dignity. People were awed by its extreme height. But they were also somewhat scared of it. On the ground, its circumference covered an area as large as Paridhi's bedroom. If one stood beneath the tree and looked up, it seemed as if its branches would cover the whole sky. At the bottom there was a small cluster of plants—toroi, bhekhuri-tita, curry leaves and many other unknown greens and weeds. Paridhi used to collect from there the dried skin of the fat bhol gourds for scrubbing her body while taking a bath. Sometimes she found broken eggshells of bortokolas, cranes, underneath. At times she even found dead chicks on the ground and her eyes filled with tears. The place also had many termite hills and in between them, monitors roamed around without fear.

Wasn't she scared of sitting there alone? When she recalled it today, Paridhi was surprised at herself. Juroni was scared of going there and warned her to stay away. Her mother did not even allow her to sit at the base of a Bokul flower tree in front of their house telling her, 'Girls shouldn't sit there. It's the abode of burha-dangaria., the demi-god. Juroni also said that a spirit lived in that simolu tree. But Paridhi did not care; she felt a thrill running through her veins when she sat at the base of the tree. She lost herself trying to unravel the mysteries of nature.

Perhaps it was also because when problems push a person to a lonely corner, only nature unquestioningly offers a cool place for them to get away from it all. Where is there scope for fear then? When she saw the huge cranes spreading their wings mournfully at the loss of their babies, Paridhi felt like hiding under for safety.

Often she asked herself, can the explorer in a man—ever-ready to unravel its mysteries—be lonely in the lap of beautiful nature? She was convinced it could not be. Even if no one was around, he could converse with the sky above. He could confide in the stars about his innermost thoughts. He could even share his sorrows with the clouds above. And, in the company of trees, another kind of conversation takes place.

But sometimes, even that much was not allowed. If a girl was open-minded only nature welcomed her with open arms, not people. Many tongues were ready to pronounce the words 'not done'. And many hands waited with fetters to bind the feet that wanted to take off.

"Are you mad to sit under the Simolu tree at midday like that?" her mother scolded her one day.

"Why, what's the problem?"

"Don't ask. Even adults are afraid to go there, and

you...?" her mother took a deep breath and continued, "Men can be more dangerous than the evil spirits. You're growing up. Those days of roaming around on your own are over. Keep yourself safe when you go outside. Shontu-da saw you and has reported it to me. Had your father seen you, your back couldn't have been saved from his stick today."

Paridhi was surprised at the hard tone her mother had taken.

"You talk about safety beyond the house, but can you save yourself from the evil spirit at home?" Paridhi retaliated.

She was not sure how her mother interpreted her words.

"You talk too much these days," was all that she said. But Paridhi heard the loud grumbling when she went to pick up the washed utensils kept upturned on the bamboo rack to dry.

Afterwards, however, she smiled to herself. Seeing her sitting under the fabled Simolu tree, people might have surmised that the evil spirit had got her.

At a little distance from there was the village cremation ground. The bodies could have been turned to ashes, but people said the souls kept floating in the air and rested on the tree. People had never seen such a huge simolu tree; they revered and feared it in equal measure. There was also talk going on that at night many unearthly sounds were heard from that place. Forget nights, even during the day the timid were afraid to go there. Underneath that tree one day was found the body of an almost skeletal Tilottama Das. Even in life she looked ghost-like, but in death she chose the base of the tree as her last resting place. Some claimed that from then on, they could hear the sound of a woman weeping from the branches of the tree. Others even said they saw her walking around the tree wearing a white dress.

Paridhi too saw the woman in a white dress roaming around the tree. But she was not Tilottama. People who saw her thought she was a ghost, but she was not. She was very much a living person. Often, she was seen getting down from the train. She always carried a bundle of clothes and kept her face covered like a new bride. People did not know what she looked like. After seeing her around for a few days, she came to know that that mysterious woman prescribed medicine for sexual diseases. Her bag contained many herbal medicines. She sold them around in the villages and in the afternoon left the place. She searched for herbs under the Simolu tree, herbs that she needed to prepare her medicines.

One day, Paridhi saw her at the platform from a distance as she waited for the train. At that exact moment, a strong breeze from behind unsettled the long end of the sador covering the woman's face. Paridhi almost jumped up. The face hidden under the sador was not like a human face—it looked like something made up of lumps. One side of her cheeks was almost absent. Underneath the eye, the flesh of her cheek was swollen like a gout-infested ankle and hung down to her neck.

Paridhi felt like running away. But then their eyes met. The woman was trying to smile at her. Without knowing why she felt compelled to do this, Paridhi started walking towards her. The woman now covered her face with the sador and said, "People are scared to look at my face. Aren't you afraid, my dear?"

"No," Paridhi lied. She sat near her and asked hesitantly, "What's happened to you?"

"Perhaps I had sinned without knowing. Otherwise why would the Lord punish me like this?"

"I don't think it's a sin that's done it, *aita*! It must be due to some disease. You should see a doctor."

The woman smiled at the suggestion. Instead, she asked Paridhi about her family. She liked the woman's soft voice and the sincerity it expressed, and without any hesitation she told her about herself. Even about her father. The train arrived and the woman got up. When the train began gathering speed, she asked the woman, shouting over the sound of the engine, "Is there any medicine to cure my father of drinking?"

The woman did not hear her. The sound of the speeding train's wheels crashed into Paridhi's ears.

12

"You know, yesterday three people came in a golden boat to take me away."

"And then?"

"The house was surrounded by water on all sides. Those men wore clothes as white as the wings of a crane. They called me from the boat—Come, it's time for you to go. I said, 'But how can I? All the doors and windows are shut.' Then I woke up."

Paridhi listened to her uncle without saying anything. He continued, "I don't think I have very many days left. Please inform the relatives if they want to see me for the last time."

Paridhi's eyes filled up. And her mother's too. She pulled the oroni over her head with due respect to her late husband's elder brother, and said softly, "Why are you saying like this? You will be fine. Now drink this water."

She tried to feed him the ORS mixed water as he sat leaning on a pillow on the bed. He protested but Paridhi insisted, "You haven't had anything since the morning. Where will you get the strength?"

Of late, he was losing interest in any kind of food. He said he did not find taste in anything. Paridhi remembered that not very long ago, if he was not served tea or lunch on time, he would lose his temper. During the day, he asked for tea quite a few times. If he had his lunch at 12 o'clock, one and half hours later he would ask for a meal again. When reminded that he had already had his lunch, he would ask suspiciously, "Are you sure?" After wrapping up her chores in the kitchen, when her mother wanted to rest a bit, he'd ask for tea again. If it took a little while he would shout, "I don't exist in this household. You don't care for me at all!"

Sometimes, both mother and daughter lost their tempers too. After all, they were only human. Even their patience ran out at times. But eventually they adjusted to the situation. Her uncle too simmered down.

Paridhi realised long ago that a home does not remain a home unless you adjust and help each other out in times of need. An uneasy atmosphere keeps the house on tenterhooks. In the absence of love and respect for each other, resentment brews and breaks up families. In the village now, hardly a few houses where extended families lived remained. Strange, as that was once the norm. People had a myriad excuses to move out. The courtyards in front of the houses which were once hubs for addas lay empty now. Her uncle told her that back in the day, if somebody died, the people of the village took care of everything for the post-death rituals and let the family mourn undisturbed. The same was true for weddings too. People did not need to rent chairs and tables for the invitees, they were simply supplied by the neighbours from their own houses.

In their own case too, at one time people often visited her uncle. He used to be very active in the village's social life. Even the young men approached him for advice on forthcoming programmes in the village. Though old and burdened with the sadness of losing his dear son to an unknown destiny, her uncle still took interest in such activities. Nowadays, hardly anyone visited him anymore. A few who were regulars had themselves left this world.

Paridhi arranged the pillow to make her uncle more comfortable. In her bedroom, she switched on the computer. Bondeep had given her a new book to type. Opening Adobe Pagemaker, she selected the file and connected the Dongle with the Ramdhenu script. Her fingers ran rapidly on the keyboard. She had to hurry to finish the book; the book fair was not that far away.

Sunflower; the name of Bondeep's publication house.

Now the sunflower smiled brightly for him, though some time ago it was about to wilt. Bondeep now enjoyed the flower of success blooming for him at last. He dared to dream again. Paridhi too felt happy that her beloved had now solid ground to stand on. There was a time when the little boy cried because he could not afford a mere ten rupees to buy a children's magazine. Now, he was publishing books by well-known writers. When she heard

Bondeep talking about his deprived childhood, she felt like crying. In her mind's eyes she could see a little boy sitting on a bus and looking longingly at the rack of magazines at the bus stand. Even when the bus was on its way, he craned back at the magazine rack for as long as the eyes could see.

His letters to her gave her a glimpse of the misery which was a part of his growing up years. Even though he wrote of happy things to distract her from her loneliness, the memory of those incidents seeped through the pages. He wrote about colours he did not know, and people he did not recognise with their chameleon exteriors, their shades changing often.

Hunger and tears were his constant companions in those years. When he and his brother slept exhausted, their mother sat by them singing a lullaby in the dark and wept silently. There were many days and nights like these. Yet, at one time their father had a lot of land. Some unknown disease took him away suddenly. So the farmer's family starved. Their uncles pretended as if they did not notice anything. "How can people be so cruel?" Bondeep had written.

His mother tried to survive by selling areca nut and betel leaves from the kitchen garden and somehow managed to buy schoolbooks and notebooks for her sons. She aged prematurely. On their return from school, when other boys went to play football in the field, Bondeep and his brother spread a hessian mat on the road to sell tamul-paan. The mosquito bites made their young legs erupt into small bumps. Yet they did not protest, they waited for customers. If by chance they managed to have an egg for dinner one day, it felt like a festival. In such circumstances, wasn't buying a magazine a luxury?

While Bondeep was studying for his B.Sc degree, he managed the cost by giving tuition to students. Though a science student, he was attracted to literature. Even in the face of endless poverty, he bought books and magazines to appease his hunger. After his graduation, he reluctantly gave up the idea for post-graduation and took a job in a small press. He nursed a dream—"Those who want to, can". At every moment, his inner voice stoked him, "Live with your head held high." That voice led him to the city. Life was not easy. After a long day's labour, when he returned to the tiny room he had rented, he wondered often, "Can I survive?" He worked as a salesman in a publication house. Then followed days of numerous hurdles, many ups and downs. He also gathered the experience of coming across the true nature of people behind their façades. But he did not lose hope. And now, his Sunflower enterprise was flourishing.

One day, as he was talking about his childhood, Bondeep had asked her, "Have you ever seen a painting on the wall in somebody's house, of a little boy with his cheeks drenched in tears?"

Without waiting for her answer, he had pointed to his chest and said, "It's here, I always carry it within me."

Paridhi removed the hand tenderly from his chest and

holding him tight pleaded, "Please forget about the tears. Please let me stay there instead."

Bondeep held her. Kissing her tenderly he said, "Don't worry. You are the queen who rules here. And in this land…" he hid his face in her breasts as he said, "And here I am the king."

"Oh! How you do go on!" Paridhi pushed him away shyly, but he held her tight again.

It feels nice to be held captive by someone, Paridhi thought at times as she smelt his nearness. At these moments, she forgot all her worries, her sadness. Only colours of happiness danced around her.

As she was typing, Paridhi stopped suddenly. A particular word's spelling confused her. She pulled up the dictionary from the table. As she turned the pages a dry rose petal slipped out from one of them. She picked it up. It was her childhood hobby. It still was. Juroni used to put a bidyapaat, the leaf associated with bidya, knowledge, and Goddess Saraswati, in her schoolbooks. Yet the marks in her exams could barely touch the pass mark of 30.

Ah, Juroni!

Yesterday when she went to the bazaar, she saw her friend from a distance, hunched over the sewing machine. She looked as vivacious as ever. It was quite in contrast to the girl she'd seen a few days ago. Then, her ears were bare of earrings, her eyes sans the usual eyeliner, the lips without lipstick. She sat immobile like a stone. She seemed to have lost her voice too.

"He got married. To a girl of his parents' choice," she said at long last.

Juroni was not talking about the 'nincompoop', she was talking about a new friend with whom she had become close quickly enough after meeting through Facebook. A few days earlier, she had confided in Paridhi, "At last I've met my wrestler hero. If I am with him, I don't care about anything, I am happy." Her long earrings danced as she smiled.

This was before she saw his updated 'status' on Facebook. Her dreams shattered. For the next few days, she did not open her shop and stopped communicating with anyone. She was in deep sorrow. She slept till late in the morning. Those in the household who took advantage of her earning hurled barbs at her sharper than spikes.

But Juroni could not sit around moping for long. Paridhi knew her. She was not one to run away from painful reality. She could not stay away from the machine that ensured her independence. So once again, the wheels of the machine gathered speed. Fast, faster. Her face was adorned with more make-up than the usual today, Paridhi observed, and felt reassured.

Juroni liked painting her face; Paridhi stuck to paper. And some people like to paint other peoples' lives. They are the ones who work without any self-interest to help others give shape to their colourful dreams.

Could Paridhi ever forget the person who understood her deep yearning for colour and helped her realise her dream? Never. He was the tall man with a strong body whose complexion was the shade of the mellow gomari tree bark that took on a special tint as the orange of the setting sun touched it. He was the new stationmaster at their village. They had never seen such a handsome stationmaster in their life.

One day, Paridhi and Juroni were walking on the railway track, each on a parallel line. Their bodies balancing on the narrow track looked like two flowering plants trembling in the wind. The stationmaster came out from his quarter and smiled at them. Then he called them. He asked them their names and what they liked.

Paridhi answered promptly—painting.

From that day onwards, Paridhi met her Station-khura, Station Uncle, almost every day. In a very short time, their friendship grew because Station-khura too loved paintings. He told Paridhi many stories about lines and drawings—and colours.

Perhaps he glimpsed in her eyes the shadow of a thick mist covering her dreamland—a field golden with ripening paddy. Her father had compelled Paridhi to think that people laid thorns in other people's paths. They built insurmountable hills for others.

But her Station-khura made her think otherwise.

That people can generously open paths for others. That people can teach others to fly.

"Have you heard about Leonardo da Vinci?"

"Yes."

"Michaelangelo?"

"Yes, yes."

"Nicolas Poussin?"

"No, I haven't. Who was he?"

"A famous French painter. He ushered in a new stream to the French art world. You can see his priceless paintings and sketches in the Louvre Museum in Paris."

He told her about many more artists. Paridhi's little brain did not have the capacity to hold all the information. Yet she felt a great attraction to all those artists.

"And do you know about Rembrandt? Ah, Rembrandt van Rijn—how beautiful were his strokes! How expressively he created a world of light and shadows! Do you know Paridhi, he has left behind fifty to sixty self-portraits."

When he told her about famous painters, Stationkhura did not take into account her young age. He spoke unceasingly as his eyes rested on the setting sun beyond the railway track. From Neelpawan, Benu Mishra, Sobha Brahma, Ganesh Pyne, Raja Ravi Varma, Rabindranath to Van Gogh, Paul Gauguin, Cezanne, he introduced them all to Paridhi. He showed her his file which was full of cuttings of paintings by the famous painters. He had collected them from newspapers and magazines which carried articles on them.

It was a whole new world for Paridhi. She could not have enough of it. Like the sunflowers in Van Gogh's painting, her dreams also bloomed. The stars came down to her from his "The Starry Night." The horses of Maqbool Fida Husain galloped at full speed in her dreams.

A little girl is leaning on a coarse concrete wall. Next to her is a lush green bush on a flowerpot. The girl's golden hair matches the colour of the frock she wears, complete with puffed sleeves, bordered with blue. In her left hand, she is holding a jet-black cat. She has covered the cat with a golden wrap. Her pink lips show that she is saying something to the cat tenderly. The forefinger of her right hand is pointing upwards to a hanging bamboo cage. Inside, there is a yellow bird. The cat inspects it intently.

She had borrowed that painting from Station-khura. It was still pasted on her scrap book. Thinking about it, Paridhi suddenly wanted to see it again. She pushed her chair back and got up and pulled out the ancient tin trunk from underneath her cot. Many things were piled there; they were mostly sentimental things but did not have any monetary value. For her though, the trunk was a treasure box. She rummaged through it, brought out the scrapbook and turned its pages.

One page had designs in dry flowers, another had

drawings of creepers, one had butterflies drawn at the top of the page while another had clusters of flowers at the bottom. In the empty pages she wrote down her thoughts, her desires, a few lines from her favourite songs, or lines from poems or a favourite book.

Books were the other companions that filled her insecure adolescence. After Anuja khuri went away, she borrowed books from the village library a few youths had set up. Once, when she went to return a book, a young man who was reading there called her, "Please listen."

He was the only one in the library at that time.

"Yes?" Paridhi was about to leave but turned to look at him.

"I'd like to speak to you."

"About what?" Paridhi was surprised. She had seen him before but had never conversed with him. Sometimes she saw him among her brother's group of friends. She only knew his name and nothing else. He was the one who one day had inspected her painting Paras showed him sitting on the verandah.

"I mean…I meant to say," the boy could not finish his sentence as the words stuck in his throat. Paridhi did not wait to hear him out. But her heart raced. What did he want to tell her? That question troubled her for a few days. And then one day Juroni brought to her a message articulating his unsaid words. Like a breeze blowing into her room. As she opened the folded paper, two sentences stood out: "I like you. I feel like talking to you about many things."

Paridhi finished her shower that day and stood in front of the mirror. She asked herself: this girl with a wheat complexion, and a plain face, could it attract someone? For a long time she stood, looking at herself.

She smiled as she remembered. Reminiscing about the adolescent girl at that juncture, she felt like shouting:

Colour, where doesn't one find you?
You're there—in the soil of the earth, in the water.
In the sky.
In the wind.
Where, where aren't you there?
You're there among people—in their bodies,
and in their hearts.
Colour, you're there beyond the darkness.

13

Only two sentences.

Just two.

Sometimes even a few words can open a whole new world. Perhaps that is why Paridhi saw her familiar world in a new way now. Is love like that? Giving one a new pair of eyes? Paridhi wondered. But she also wondered if it was really love. She was rather young to understand what love actually was. She did not know whether 'liking' was equivalent to love. But slowly, she started liking that fair, tall boy with a quiet demeanour. But she did not even dream of writing a reply to his letter. Now, when she saw him, she stole looks at his deep eyes underneath the arched eyebrows. When he smiled crookedly at her, the face remained with her.

Once, when he saw her sitting with Juroni at the station platform, he broke away from the group of boys who were enjoying their afternoon adda session. Juroni nudged her with her elbow and whispered, "See, here comes your Romeo."

"Hei you, keep quiet," Paridhi was embarrassed.

The boy stood in front them and asked softly, "How are you doing?"

"I am fine," Paridhi answered while pulling Juroni's dress to stop her from leaving them alone.

"Which book have you read last?"

"*Anuradha's Land.*"

"Yes, some laughter carries the colour of the heart," he quoted the words from the book to address her.

"Please read Arupa Patangia Kalita's *Ayananta*. A very good book. It's in our library."

Paridhi felt as if he added the last sentence to cover his uncertainty about how she would take his intrusion.

He did not have a chance to talk more. By now, the boys in his group sitting across the track were teasing him mercilessly.

Paridhi admitted to herself that she did not mind his 'intrusion'. But she was also scared. Suppose one of those boys reported her whereabouts to her father or her cousin, Shontu-da? There were many people in the village who took vicarious pleasure in making a mountain out of a molehill. And if, God forbid, it reached the ears of the middle-aged Romoni! Behind his back, villagers gave him the sobriquet Narad, the heavenly figure who carried stories from one god to another to create conflict. This man did not have anything better to do, Paridhi concluded. He was the cause of many quarrels in the village. He had at his fingertips all the village gossip—who went to whose house and why, who had an affair with whom, who was going to elope soon, in which household the husband-wife quarrelled through the night, he knew everything. He visited the houses without invitation, chewed the tamul offered to him and supplied these juicy stories to eager ears.

That one night, Prasanta beat his wife Anuja almost senseless came out from Romoni's sack of tales. When she heard it from her mother, Paridhi ran to her house. She felt very close to the beautiful woman.

That Prasanta would welcome Urvashi with open arms any day was given. The relationship was an open secret and villagers had taken it in their stride. As the days passed, they accepted Urvashi as one of them. She too regarded them as her own people. There was something about Urvashi. Her eyes, like the water of a deep pool, perhaps attracted the lovers. Her slim waist, as if drawn by an artist's stroke, must have enticed them too. The tinkling sound of her laughter hung in the air for a long time. It was difficult to ignore that sexy laughter. So how could Prasanta's eager hand stay away from this flesh-and-blood honeycomb?

But when the villagers heard that Prasanta was getting married, a big question mark hung in the air. They were even more surprised to learn that Urvashi had consented to the marriage. No one knew what was going on. The wedding was performed with the usual fanfare, complete with the bursting of crackers and rocket bombs. Nobody among the invitees could make out whether Urvashi accepted it, or whether a fire scalded her heart. A few men who secretly hankered after her attention tried to show sympathy but did not receive any encouragement from her. She behaved the same way as always, laughing at the slightest, as if nothing was amiss. The new bride also accepted her as her sister-in-law.

A few days after the wedding Juroni almost forced Paridhi to visit the house to meet the new bride. Paridhi liked her instantly. They saw her arranging books in the cabinet on top of the big bedstead she had brought as a wedding gift from her family.

So many books!

Paridhi was used to seeing new brides bringing along lots of things but not books. As her eyes eagerly ran over the titles, the new bride smiled and asked, "Do you want to read any of them?" Paridhi nodded. She selected one for Paridhi. It was *Adha Likha Dostabez,* An Unfinished Autobiography, in English by Mamoni Raisom Goswami.

That was the beginning. Paridhi finished reading and then re-read it. She felt as if she knew the writer very well. She could deeply empathise with her. Slowly, the attraction of the books and the company of Anuja-khuri drew her to the house quite often. Every two to three days, she went to the house looking for books. She fell in love with the characters in them. They seemed to take on human forms and walked around her. Absorbed in that world, she often had to face complaints from people that she did not respond to their queries. Paridhi read them secretly, fearing her father's wrath if he saw her reading something other than schoolbooks. She hid them under the mattress. When she went to return a book, Anuja-khuri discussed it with her, putting forth her own impression of that book. Paridhi was struck by her analysis and how deeply she thought about the characters.

"Life is very beautiful, you know Paridhi! Like the novels. Even more beautiful are the dreams."

When this same person said one day that she wanted to go away somewhere forever, Paridhi was dumbstruck.

"Somewhere, means?"

"Somewhere far…far away. From where nobody returns."

Anuja-khuri's voice seemed to emerge from some deep cave.

Paridhi was at a loss for words. She felt a deep sadness. It was as if a red train passed by in front of her eyes for an unknown destination.

"A heart that does not have a green shoot, where birds do not sing, how can one find shelter there and dream? And without dreams, how can you live?" Anuja-khuri was lost in a soliloquy as she gripped the rods of the window and looked beyond.

The woman with impeccable taste, who loved books and the beauty of nature, was sorely disappointed with the man who was unfamiliar with this world. Even the wedding night, when they were supposed to start a life together, fell flat. She waited, trembling in anticipation, to hear a tune she only knew about but had never heard. She was rudely hauled up from her dream-world when her new husband entered the room and told her, 'You go to sleep,' picked up a pillow from the flower-bedecked bed and went out of the room. After a few moments, the sound of somebody weeping could be heard.

It was a wedding house. Who could cry like this in a house of celebration, the new bride wondered. She once heard from someone that a mother cried when her son got married, perhaps apprehensive that she was going to lose control of the household. But it was not the cry of an old woman. Anuja was tired, hungry too, so she could not keep her eyes open for long. Eventually, the sound of weeping also stopped. She succumbed to sleep. Only the heavy breathing of two people could be heard from beyond the wall but by that time the new bride was deep asleep.

Afterwards, when she found her man by her side at night, she felt like an overflowing river, fulfilled. A river that sought to embrace the raw colours of life with its hungry tide. But even a river in spate does not like heartlessness. Prasanta did not understand the language of the river. For him, the woman only meant a lush figure to be devoured. His fingers did not have the warmth of intimacy.

Was this the reason that the woman wanted to go away?

More than anything, the reason was Urvashi. As she went about her chores, her body language changed when Prasanta was around, Anuja noticed. She also caught the strain of gossip around her. Within a month, the mature woman understood that Urvashi was not her sister-in-law after all, but the 'other woman'. Urvashi was like a fireball that tormented her all the time.

After much thought, one day Anuja decided to approach her mother-in-law. But she was in for a shock. The old woman told her coldly, "Be careful when you talk about Urvashi like this. She has come to this house much before you. She is part of the family. It's better that you accept it and maintain peace in the house. Besides, if you don't know how to control your own man, what can I do?"

Those were not just words spoken by someone but the hammering of a stone. Anuja felt her heart breaking into pieces at the attack. Pain shrouded her days and nights. The fireball destroyed her dream of becoming a flowing river of love.

"If your husband is with another woman…Oh, how terrible! How is she bearing all this? For a woman there's nothing worse that can happen."

This was how women in the village discussed Anuja-khuri's situation. They felt that she should leave for her parents' place. It was the only solution.

Anuja did protest. She asked Prasanta why he had done this to her. If he couldn't live without Urvashi, why did he make a show of marrying her? Prasanta did not have an answer. Anuja knew the fire that consumed her had also scorched Urvashi when Prasanta spent some nights with her. But Prasanta was unaffected by the twin fireballs, not a hair on his skin felt the heat.

Though Anuja decided to leave, she paused. She bore it all—the pain, the abuses, the comments. She had to. Prasanta, his mother and Urvashi treated her in a way as if it was her fault that she came to the house as a bride. When she heard about the torture, Paridhi too asked her to leave.

One day, when she went to return a book, she found that books were strewn around on the bed and the floor of Anuja-khuri's room. Some had lost the jackets. The cabinet on top of the bed did not have a single book. Anuja-khuri herself was sitting on the floor amidst the torn books and weeping. Paridhi did not have to be told what had happened. When she placed her hand on her shoulder and called out to her, the face that turned to her was full of red welts—the signature of a man's right. From the corner of her lips a thin stream of blood flowed down.

"You leave today!" Paridhi almost screamed.

She did. But it was not final. Prasanta went to fetch her a few days later and she returned. Paridhi was angry and so did not visit her for a few days. Anuja sent word through Juroni. When she came, Anuja-khuri touched her face tenderly and said, "I know, you're angry with me for coming back. But what can I do? You are young, you won't understand some of these things. Do you know what people in the family say after a girl is married off? Whether she is with the son-in-law or Yama, the God of Death, it's the same. I've now accepted that I have to live with the threat of Yama. I lost my parents at a young age. My elder brother lives separately with his family. My younger brother has his family too, but he has never scrimped on my education. He spent lavishly for my wedding too. How can I become a burden to their household again? I haven't told them anything about the living hell I am in here. I'll bear it alone. And one day when my patience will run out, I will go away somewhere far away, not to my parents' place."

"But..." Paridhi wanted to say something but stopped.

"What 'but' Paridhi?"

"Well, you yourself said once that if you don't learn from the books and emulate, there's no point reading them."

"Yes, I did. But I don't understand why you are bringing up the topic now."

"I'll tell you later," Paridhi closed the subject and left.

Back home, she took out her scrapbook and ran her eyes over the words she had copied. She paused over a particular passage. She had copied a few sentences from the book called *Na Hanyate,* It Does Not Die by Maitryee Devi.

"If someone is cruel to you and in return you treat yourself cruelly too, it doesn't make any sense. Do not lose hope, respect yourself, take yourself away from your surroundings and go deep into yourself. You will find your self will even defeat fate. Whatever the circumstances, whatever be the fate, you try to rise above it."

Sometimes Anuja even imagined herself in Urvashi's place. Though she had her lover, she could not put vermillion at the parting of her hair to establish her place as a legitimate partner. She too was suffering, she too was sharing her man with another. Was her pain less than Anuja's? She often thought of the depth of a well. Her heart felt lost in the depths as the narrow ring went down and down, getting narrower still before it ended in a small pool at the bottom. But here it did not meet cool water; it was poisoned water.

How long could she carry the poisoned water in the cave of her heart? And Urvashi? Didn't she also carry the poisoned water in the pool of her heart? In secret moments, did she imagine herself putting the vermillion in the parting of her hair? Perhaps she did and then rubbed it off—that too only in her imagination. Or was she happy with things as they were? Perhaps it was enough for her to fulfill her physical craving behind the door of her locked room. True, when Anuja thought about Urvashi like this she felt sorry for her, but at the next moment when Urvashi ill-treated her the feeling vanished. So the mental and physical torture continued.

On Sasthi, the beginning of Durga puja, Prasanta, a self-confessed devotee of the goddess, beat up Anuja until she was almost unconscious because she dared to argue with Urvashi. In the morning, when Paridhi found her bedridden and tried to give her some relief by giving her a massage, she heard Urvashi speaking mockingly within her earshot. Prasanta's mother sat calmly without reacting. From the side of the station the sound of chanting floated in the air. They were paying to goddess Shakti.

During the annual Durga puja festival, the little station near Paridhi's village took on a festive air. The villagers organised the puja at the open field near the station. Everybody took part, though the Brahmins, as usual, dominated the rituals. Much ahead of the actual festivities, accompanied by a few older members, the young men went from house to house to collect donations for the puja. From then on to Dashami, the last day, the festival lent an atmosphere of joy to their village. From the venue devotional songs were aired through the microphone. Strains of *Om Jai Jagadishya hare* filtered into every household. In the evening, during the aarati ritual, the combined sound of the big doba, the kettle drum, cymbals and conch-shells made even the non-believer feel the presence of the devi among them in her earthly abode.

Sure, there were people in the village who did not believe in the puja rituals. Not because they were atheists, but they did not believe in idols. They were Vaishanavites who followed the religion introduced by Mahapurush Sankardev. Even they bought new clothes for their children and balloons from the temporary stalls put up during the puja. However, they did not enter the pandal where the actual puja was being performed.

The village had people from different castes and ethnic groups like Koch, Kalita, Sutia, Tiwa, Keot, Brahmins, and so on. For the adolescent Paridhi, whose mind was always full of questions, the divisions created confusion. They were of the same flesh and blood, so why were they still divided into upper and lower classes?

In their backyard, there was a wooden stool for people like Matia-kai, who sat there to drink tea from a glass. The suffix *kai* was a shortened form of *kakaideu,* elder brother, which they used to address him as a show of respect for his age. But after he left, keeping the stool leaning against the wall, Paridhi's aunt poured water over it. Paridhi was used to these scenes. Daily labourer Ratiram drank tea from a glass too, not a cup as they did, and afterwards washed it and kept it on the corner of the verandah before leaving. Until the next time he visited and had tea, it remained in the same place. She saw her aunt pour black tea with salt in the glass without touching it. She heard that in her grandmother's days, things were even worse. When she poured the tea, the man from the lower caste was not allowed to touch the glass. Why? Was it possible that the blood of a lower caste man could travel up to contaminate the upper caste people? From those days to Paridhi's time, things had changed a lot, but it did not mean that the days of some privileged people sitting on an elevated place or pouring water over a used stool were totally over.

In their neighbourhood, in Joon-dada's house, because the surnames of the husband and wife did not match, three sons of the family had to be excommunicated. The sons who wore the white logun thread the Brahmins sported, by chance found it coloured by love. People of the high caste refused to let in the wind that carried that particular colour's whiff. But who could predict from which side love suddenly enters?

"Oh, all three of them ... !" the villagers lamented. And so, the house where four young men flourished together now lay almost empty; the rooms that once seemed too small for the family seemed too big now. The space widened and widened and the sighs of the old parents tried to fill up the space. The old father who was present in every wedding in the village to sing biya-naam, wedding songs, could not hold a single wedding in his own courtyard. How painful it must have been. The eldest son, Joon, was still there in the house. But people knew he too would leave one day. He would have to. And the space in the house would expand even further.

In fact, Joon had already passed the age of an eligible bachelor. He waited. But for how long could he wait? He had also promised someone to make her his companion for life. He did not hesitate to welcome her as his own, though she belonged to a lower caste. At last, he had to make a decision. He bought a small plot of land on the other side of the railway track and built a small cottage. He arranged his own wedding, without any ritual. The night before that, he slept by his mother's side. He rested his head on her breast like a little child. The woman who had to let her four sons go one by one in the name of social custom, held on to him throughout the night. At dawn, Joon told his mother, "Let me know if you need anything. And if I send word please come out of the house to the road in front."

The road between the two sides remained the same but it had become an invisible divisive line between mother and son. After Joon got married, the family had to go through a set of rituals to get rid of the 'sin.' That was the ordained custom.

Custom. Custom. Custom!

It puzzled Paridhi. People built a society and then introduced rules in order to divide society. But was it possible to bind all by so-called customs? Some broke out.

Anuja-khuri too broke out of the mold. It was the day of Bijoya Dashami. Everyone bade the devi farewell on this day until her homecoming next year. A general sadness hung in the air. On the quiet platform, Paridhi and Juroni met her for the last time. She was pulling along a big suitcase with great difficulty and a bag was hanging from her shoulders when they met her.

"I have thought a lot. I'll not return this time. I won't even go far away. My brother and sister-in-law would not shut their door on me. But I won't be a burden to them. People say my embroidery work is good. I'll design boutique sets of mekhela sador. My sister-in-law also says there's a great demand for these exclusive clothes in the city. I'll manage till these hands can work. But I'll never live like a creeper depending on others. The characters in my favourite books keep rebuking me constantly when I live like the dead. They remind me life is beautiful. Even with the ugly elements, life is still beautiful. It holds thousands of meanings. What's the use of dying little by little every day for the sake of a lecherous, unworthy man? Live for yourself."

Anuja khuri talked for a long time. Paridhi understood that characters in her favourite books gave her the strength to defy fate. After some time, the train with its red bogies arrived at the platform.

"Anuja-khuri will go away now. Forever!" The thought gave Paridhi relief, but she also felt as if a heavy stone was sitting on her chest, suffocating her. Anuja-khuri's hand waving them goodbye remained etched in her memory forever, like the cross marked on the back of the last bogie of the train. Even today, she had not forgotten Anuja-khuri's last words: "No matter that I can't be a huge tree. Even to be a neglected era tree is better. But I'll be a tree, never a creeper."

14

A butterfly was hovering over a bunch of red rongon flowers. The butterfly's inky black wings were white underneath and speckled with vermillion dots. It seemed as if it had stolen a bit of red from the Rongon flowers to decorate itself. The butterfly danced around for some time and then flew away. Another butterfly suddenly appeared and followed it. Now the couple rested on the nohorumalati creeper. The plant was full of white malati flowers tinged with a light purple colour. It exuded a faint aroma of garlic when rubbed between the palms; that's where it got its name—nohoru, garlic. The drooping, leaf-covered flowers looked like garlands. Who painted a light purple on them so lovingly? A few bumblebees hummed around. Some entered deep into the flower's core. Emerging after sucking the nectar, their black heads showed off crowns of yellow pollen. Last year, when Nabaneeta had visited her at this time of the year, she clicked photos of the flower enthusiastically. In any case, she was obsessed with taking snaps. She was almost ten years older to Paridhi but looked as young as her. Restless and effervescent, always dressed in a pair of jeans and a top, her eyes lined with kohl—that was Nabaneeta. Be it in summer or winter, she never tied her soft, wavy hair. Her husband was a successful businessman and she enjoyed a luxurious lifestyle. Yet, she wrote with great empathy about people's sufferings. How was it possible for her to imagine such situations, the writers' group that Paridhi belonged to often puzzled over it.

Paridhi for one knew that Nabaneeta was bored with the kind of life she was leading as a rich man's wife. She dressed elegantly, carried herself well, but she never seemed haughty or aloof. Rather than flitting around in the party circuit, she preferred spending time with ordinary people. She liked sitting with them on a ramshackle bamboo bench and sharing the potatoes and yams they roasted over an open fire.

Once Paridhi had to stay back in Guwahati where she had gone on an errand and spent the night at Nabaneeta's house at her insistence. In the palatial house, where she sat in the bedroom fit for a princess, Nabaneeta had confided, "There was a time when I dreamt of a house of my own but today all these luxuries fail to make me happy. Because I am not sure if my other self is happy."

Nabaneeta's husband was not there that day. He had gone abroad. In any case, he was hardly home. He was not that concerned about what Nabaneeta was doing with her time. At first, he had objected to her taking up the job of an assistant editor in the magazine. She didn't need the money as she lacked for nothing in material life. Eventually, however, he gave in. Anyhow, he did not have time to read what his wife was writing.

"I remember a time when he was madly in love with me. A single teardrop from my eyes used to make him feel miserable. He didn't have much money in his purse, but he kept me rich with dreams for the future. How intensely he clung to me for support. But was it an illusion or true love? At least it seemed true love to me at that time. If the heart accepts something as true, then it seems so. At that time, I didn't hear any inner voice telling me otherwise. But why do I hear it today? Why can't I be reassured? During the courting period, we wanted to be together all the time, but didn't have many opportunities. But that separation created its own web of romantic imagination. And now, we don't have to worry, we can be together anytime. What is lacking is that intense desire. Now the lips don't seek out each other hungrily, the fingers don't reach out with desire for touch. Our bodies, our minds, are not where butterflies fly searching for colour. You know Paridhi, I feel completely abandoned sometimes. I try to climb up from the pit but then I slide down again."

Nabaneeta took a long breath and then continued: "A man should reassure a woman from time to time that she is important to him. He should know that this expression of love is valuable to her—and for him too. A woman loved is like a lighted wick in an earthen lamp that spreads the calm light to others around her."

Nabaneeta loved the colour purple. That day, she breathed in with deep appreciation the faint garlic smell of the flowers. She told Paridhi that the name of the plant was Rachel. She confessed that she felt envious of the name. To Paridhi, on the other hand, the name immediately brought to mind something else—Van Gogh's self-portrait after he had cut off his ear. It is said that he sliced off his ear for lady love, Rachel, and later presented it to her wrapped in a handkerchief. Was it why Nabaneeeta envied the name, Paridhi wondered idly.

Near the flowering rachel creeper hung strands of graceful kopou orchids from a big tree. Paridhi could hear birds tweeting from there now. She craned her neck and tried to recognise the bird. Was it the bhodorkoli, in her black and white attire? Or was it the tiny tiposi? Her eyes now strayed to the rose bushes in front of the verandah. She picked up the spade lying on the heap of dry cow-dung.

At that moment, she heard the main gate to the road opening. She turned her head to see who it was. It was Joydev's mother. The woman's eyes were red and swollen. Without waiting for Paridhi to ask her anything, she informed her that from now on she won't be able to supply milk. Yesterday, when she was at her brother's house, Joydev had sold off the cow in her absence. For the first time, Paridhi found her expressing anger at her son. Her voice broke. She then left abruptly. Paridhi could still hear her choked voice. She kept looking at the poor woman. As she reached the gate, she covered her face with the sador, perhaps to hide her tears from public view.

"Even Yama doesn't take him."

The woman's words rang in her ears. Yes, Yama had visited Joydev a couple of times but had turned away. Once, when a terrible stomach pain wracked him, and another time when he vomitted blood, then next when he broke his skull by hitting something. There was also the time when he lay in bed for days on end as his body refused to move. He could not even go to the bathroom for ablutions. God knows how the old woman gathered the strength to lift him up. When neighbours went to enquire after him, Joydev said gratefully, "Ah, my poor mother is looking after me very well."

After a few days Joydev was well enough to head to the liquor den and harass his mother again. Paridhi empathised with his mother's pain. She had heard that these days the woman had found a new way of hiding things. She could not afford to buy a gas cylinder now. To concoct a makeshift kitchen, she built a shed with bamboo poles and a few tin sheets for a roof. She dug a hole to act as a stove to cook the meals. She gave up asking her son and chopped off the thick stalks of the bamboo for the poles herself. Joydev helped with putting up the tin sheets, though. One day, one of the sheets disappeared too. In that half a shed, Joydev's mother dug a few holes and filling polythene bags with rice, potato, tea leaves etc. she covered them up with earth so that Joydev could not find them. But what could she do with the cow? It was not possible to hide it.

Neither Joydev, nor his mother, could escape the

battlefield of this world, Paridhi thought, as she dug the earth around the roots of the rose bushes. Could Nabaneeta escape from pain even though she wrote about the sufferings of others? Nah, the pain of living affected everybody. Like herself too. There were many battles she had fought with others throughout her life, and with herself too. On top of that, many problems, big and small, piled on her. When she tried to share these with Bondeep, he recited an old Russian proverb, "When life's problems or dangers knock at your door, open the door wide."

Paridhi was resting after having finished typing the manuscript of the new book. It was urgent, she knew, as the book fair was right round the corner. Sunflower Publication was launching quite a few books by well-known writers this time. Bondeep had also asked her to put together her published stories and compile them into an anthology. She did not pay much attention to the proposal and said she would do so eventually, sometime in the future. In the past week, Bondeep had called her only once a day. Even then, the conversations were about how busy he was. Sometimes she was determined not to take his call. What was the point? But as she folded the clothes on the clotheshorse, she felt like sending him a message. Clicking on the 'create message' option she wrote: "The light of your love gives me strength to walk, to dream. If that love wanes, my life's colour will lose its vibrancy."

She regretted it immediately as she sent the message. He must be sitting now at the desk working with the designer, planning a book jacket.

The message tone came alive. Bondeep: "Nothing has changed, my love hasn't waned either. Everything is the same. Only, very, very busy. After the book fair, we will go together to some place, somewhere you like." Paridhi read the message again and again. It was true. They had not gone anywhere together in a long time. At those times, when they wanted to sit together alone somewhere and talk, there were thousands of problems. Now, nobody was there to object, but where was the time? After the book fair they would go to Hoolock Gibbon Sanctuary near Jorhat in upper Assam, she decided. Mayur had invited her many times. Suddenly she remembered—he had requested her to paint a few pebbles with butterflies. On the day of his book launch, a few foreigners were expected to be there. He wanted to present them each a decorated pebble. He was ready to pay for her work. When he asked her how much he should pay she had protested. But he scolded her sternly, "Why should I take it gratis? And why should you too give them away for free? I know art cannot be evaluated on the price-scale but there's a value to your time and labour. Do you know, these painted stones are sold at sky-high prices abroad?"

When Paridhi uploaded some of her works on her

Facebook page, many had offered to buy them. But she had hesitated; they were dear to her heart and she did not feel like handing them to others. Each carried a piece of her.

She went to check her beloved stones. They were sleeping inside a huge basket with a cover she had bought in an exhibition. She looked at them fondly. As soon as she opened the cover, it seemed as if they wanted to jump out on to her lap. Their bodies, hardened by the weariness of hundreds of years, seemed to sing a soft song to her. An admirer of her stories, Rajdeep, had once commented on her Facebook page: "Precious treasures. Perhaps they wake up at night as dolls and sing lullabies to you."

He was right. For her, they were not just stones but living beings. They laughed, they cried, they talked to her. The basket hummed with their whispers. She felt like picking up each and holding it fondly in her palm. She wanted to listen to their soft voice speaking from inside the hard shell.

And why not, Paridhi mused. Man and stones—their relationship goes eons back. Stones have been living close to humans during different stages, first as a hunting tool, and sometimes as a medium to reflect expressions. People wrote on stones in their own language. Sculptors shaped stones into idols of gods and goddesses. Stone temples are abundant in the land. From Konark's Surya temple built by Narasingha, to Mahabalipuram, to Sanchi's Ashokan pillar and Khajuraho's Yogini temple, Indian civilisation is replete with instances of excellence in stone architecture and sculptures.

Who says stones are mute?

From one era to another, the stones continue to tell many stories.

Paridhi somehow could relate to stories on stones told in the classics. Perhaps man wanted to etch his stories on stones to last for ages after he disappeared from earth. Perhaps the stones truly knew about man's dreams and sorrows. When she was young, Paridhi had heard the story of Tulasi, the basil plant, and how she turned into a stone. She often saw her elderly aunt reading the pages of a slim book called tulasi-akhyan. It described how a stone was born of the grief-stricken Tulasi. Lord Vishnu had stolen her virginity, taking the form of Shankhasur. In her grief, Tulasi gave up her life at the feet of Vishnu. From that still body came out the gondoki salagram stone and from her hair was born the basil plant. According to a legend, salagram, a roundish pebble perforated on one side and worshipped as an emblem of Lord Vishnu, is found near the Gondoki river in north India.

Paridhi also remembered a play that was enacted on their village stage once. It was about a princess. A victim of a lecherous, cruel man, the beautiful princess Pushpabhadra jumped into the river. Mother river took her to her bosom tenderly; the princess had now turned into a stone. From then on, Pushpabhadra was known as Shilabhadra.

After watching the play, that night Paridhi dreamt of a slim girl running naked, frightened to her core, as if someone was chasing her. Both sides of the road were lined with vile men laughing at her plight. Their vulgar utterings made her even more scared. She ran and ran.

She woke with a start in the dead of night and drank thirstily from the bottle next to her bed. She was surprised—why did she dream that dreadful dream? Who was that girl with the terrified eyes?

Now that terrifying dream chased her every day. Each morning when she opened the newspaper, she found that girl looking at her from its pages. So many Pushpabhadras lie silently, turned into Shilabhadras at the bottom of the river.

And men stand silently as witnesses to the naked truth.

15

A firefly was going round and round in the dark room, blinking off and on. Paridhi could not sleep. She watched it intensely. Her mother lay next to her. Her breathing was soft and even, she was in deep sleep. The never-ending household chores during the day made her tired and so she did not have trouble falling and staying asleep. In the faint light of the room, Paridhi looked at her mother. She looked much older than her age.

It was but natural; she had gone through so many stressful years. If Paridhi were not by her, how would she have managed on her own? Her elderly uncle might pass away any day. Whenever she dreamt of starting a new life with Bondeep, her mother's pitiful face came up in her mind. Would it be better if she stayed on with her mother? Or she could maybe bring her along to her new home? But she was not sure if Bondeep's mother would welcome the idea of her mother staying with her. Sometimes when Paridhi came across her in a wedding or some social function, she inadevertently cringed. The way the woman looked at her was not friendly at all. Perhaps she was afraid that she would have to stay away from her younger son due to Paridhi. Her family could never, or would never, publicly accept her as the daughter-in-law of their house. Paridhi also thought it a great misfortune that she would not be welcomed as a member of her beloved's family. Despite that, Paridhi felt somewhat close to the lady because she was, after all, Bondeep's mother.

Sometimes, however, she could not help feeling betrayed: 'Why am I ignored like this? People say that I have some good qualities but in their eyes I am always one step behind a Brahmin girl even if she is not talented.'

Paridhi came to know through the grapevine that Bondeep's mother was searching for a Brahmin girl for her son. She lost her equilibrium when she heard this and took it out on Bondeep. At these moments, he would take her hand in his and declare, "You are inside me like a tree with deep roots. You are the only one who can make me hold on to something. Nobody can keep me engaged like you. You don't even know what kind of power you have over me. I feel like laughing out loud when I hear that you are afraid I will belong to someone else. My mother may go on looking for a girl for me but as far as I am concerned, Paridhi, you are my life, my breath."

Life.

Breath.

But everything is so uncertain in life.

Like a new businessman foraying into an uncertain future, one has to walk through life with measured steps.

Paridhi knew that till her uncle was alive her place in this house was assured. Shontu-dada must have already made plans for the house after his father's demise. Currently, he lived in a house provided by his rich father-in-law, but he was planning on buying a flat in the city. Paridhi understood all this by his body language even though he did not verbally articulate it. Though their house was in the village, it was near the highway and would fetch a good bargain price. Eventually, the house would be divided again. This had already happened once during her father's time. Paridhi and her mother would be confined to two rooms at best. They would have to accept it without protest.

The prospect made her feel a little unsettled. This was the house where she spent twenty-six years of her life, weathering many storms. In this house, she sometimes writhed in pain as if sitting on hot sand, but sometimes also felt happy at small little things. This was where she got introduced to many aspects of life. She started painting and writing in this house. She had planted flowers in its garden. Whatever be the state of the house, it was here that her heart found a restful nook.

The firefly was still flying about, flaring up like an iridescent, small, yellow flower. Perhaps it had lost its way. Like Paridhi now. Its intermittent light somehow reminded her of Paras.

Oh, if he were here today! In her absence he would

have taken good care of her mother and ensured a safe shelter for her.

That boy had disappeared but then came back. Why did you have to take him away again? Paridhi was not sure to whom she addressed these words. She did not have a god to whom she could complain. An unseen hand that touched her head when she was at a loss. That's all, beyond that she could not find a god to believe in.

That day, people in the house were waiting with bated breath for his return. Paras had not turned up in the last three days. True, sometimes he stayed over in his friend's place for the night after a performance, but that was for a night or two at best. So, at first, his mother did not worry. But after three days worry began to creep in. Everybody in the village looked for him but he was nowhere to be found. The possibility that something untoward had happened cast a shadow over them. There was a reason too. Paras and a few of his friends tried hard to shut down the bhati-khana. The boys in their twenties were hated by the policemen who took a bribe from the owner to look the other way. The drunkards did so too. Was he a victim of revenge killing? People knew that Paras was at the forefront of this campaign.

Days passed. Fear escalated. Paridhi's mother almost

stopped eating. Her body shrank. Even her father, who more often than not shouted at him, sat quietly in a corner. Paridhi felt the earth beneath her shaking. She shed tears recalling the conversations her brother had had with her, sharing his dreams with her while sitting at the railway platform. Her bordeuta suffered too. He regarded Paras as his own son. Every day he waited, like others in the afternoon, at the gates of their houses, for their dear ones to return from the city after the day's work, but he was disappointed.

The world seemed to lose all meaning for Paridhi. Her face, her walk, all reflected dejection. One day, seeing her like this, Station-khura told her, "My dear, at your age it's not right to go around moping like this. There's no end to man's pain and suffering. Temporarily it may go, but it will come again. We have to accept this truth and move on. There's nothing permanent in life, we haven't come to stay here forever. So try to live in this earth with energy, with zest for life. Nature will herself show you her varied shades. Worship the true colour of life. Try to find pearls in the caves of suffering. Choose the right path, and then walk confidently."

Station-khura's words were like a streak of sunshine for her. She started to paint again. He taught her to draw with great care. Within a very short time, she learnt the basics of painting. She did not care that some people passed snide remarks at her for going to a newcomer to learn painting; in fact, her desire to learn only grew stronger, spurred her on.

Paridhi also learnt many things about paintings and a painter's world from her Station-khura. She did not practise it, but she learnt about oil colour, acrylic, mix-media, fresco, scroll, and so on.

While explaining Tempera paintings, he told her, "Whatever colour time smears on life, the inner white in you will keep it beautiful."

Paridhi understood. White. It connotes light.

"The meaning of tempera is to make it strong," he had explained.

Paridhi had drawn a small sun with a thin red line on the wall of her bedroom. One day she painted within it a spectrum of colours as taught by her teacher. More than two hundred years ago, a French scientist named Chevreul had discovered the hidden meaning of colours. Looking at it, divided into warm and cool colours, Paridhi often mused that human life was also like the spectrum—warm and cool, moving in eternal circles.

Station-khura was an art aficionado. Knowledge about the days of Guru Sankardev in the Middle Ages when the art of painting flourished in Assam, to modern times, Indian painting styles and sculptures as well as European ones, all were on his fingertips. Though an important exam was hovering ahead, Paridhi still spent time listening to him. The lives of great painters stirred her mind and their paintings, her soul. When she sat stupefied looking at a clipping of Salvador Dali's *Persistence of Memory,* her Station-khura talked about Surrealism. It must be some new style of painting, Paridhi thought, all this too esoteric for her.

Station-khura tried to make it simpler for her. "In the early 20th century, between the two World Wars in France, the philosophy of Surrealism influenced contemporary painting and literature which was especially evident in poetry and songs. In the subconscious mind reality shows up in an apparently illogical and irrelevant way. These images are reflected in Surrealism. Surrealist painters composed poems in the same way. There was hardly any difference between the two—poems and paintings. Just think of Bhupen Hazarika's songs, how the stanzas become like reels of films. I think there are few Surrealists like him among us."

Maqbul Fida Husain, it is said, had once commented, "Bhupen, I paint with a paint brush and colour. You not only paint, you compose poems, you write lyrics and you sing. You are a double Surrealist—you paint with your lyrics, which can be seen with the mind."

Today, Paridhi could understand the meaning of those lyrics; their images floated into her mind:

My silent night
Woven without words
A blue shawl
In its soft fold
A breath like a song
And a love alive

Paintings moved her and so she made it a point to visit art exhibitions in the town even if she had other commitments. She considered painters the most talented and enviable personalities on earth. Because they knew how to reflect people's feelings with their paintbrushes, and, they knew too how to bring alive the beauty of nature.

Rembrandt's *The Storm of the Sea of Galilee*. Who would say it was just a storm created by paintbrushes? Looking at it, didn't one feel as if one was witnessing a real storm? Was Leonardo's *Monalisa* only made of acrylic? Wasn't she a flesh-and-blood woman? And that painting one often come across hanging on walls in many drawing rooms—Paridhi did not know the artist's name—of a freshly bathed woman, her clothes clinging to her still-wet body as she leaned on a post with her hand on her mouth and her eyes looked far away, lost in intense thought. Wasn't she lifelike enough for one to want to touch her arms and ask, "What are you thinking about?"

A painter could capture the sun in his hand, Paridhi mused often.

Her Station-khura had shown her a few paintings he had made in his youth. They were not done in bright colours but in shades of brown, the colours of the soil. They were about people who eked out a living through hard labour. True, they did not draw the eyes instantly, but there was a rhythm of life there. And there was a reverence.

After the final exam, Paridhi started practising with watercolour the way Station-khura taught her. Her hands were now getting steadier. Her father still tried to stop her, but she did not care. Now if he objected, she dared to answer back. But on the whole, she tried to distance herself from her father as much as possible. One day, after he passed a slang comment involving her and Bondeep, and raised his hand about to slap her, she caught his hand midway and told him sternly, "If I have to be told something, bor-ta will tell me, my mother will tell me. Not you."

She walked away. Her father might have heard something about Bondeep's interest in her from a gossipmonger. He often met her at the station; they talked. Paridhi did not think it wrong. Sometimes they talked about Paras. She could not hold her emotions back sometimes. He tried to console her. She liked to think of him alive somewhere. One day he would return. One day his story of a little child would come alive through celluloid.

Once, while chatting, Paridhi pointed to the simolu tree on the other side of the railway track and told him, "I love that tree very much."

"And me?"

Paridhi looked down at her toes. She could not answer.

"Let's go there," he said.

Paridhi looked at him in surprise. All these days, everybody had warned her about going there. Even Juroni, who roamed around the village and the jungles did not agree to go with her if she asked her to. Paridhi did not hesitate further. He kept his cycle near the waiting room of the station, locked it and followed her. When she crossed the road from the railway track, the spiky little seeds of the bonguti plants stuck to her dress. The earth beneath their feet was parched in the hot Chhot month.

Only a few weeks ago the branches of the simolu tree were full of flowers that looked like red cups; now they were bare. At the base of the tree were gathered several of the seeds that had now broken open. Paridhi opened one and took out the tuft of cottonwool from inside. She liked opening the seeds like this. The white cottonwool, like little specks of soft clouds, floated over their heads. She sat at the base of the tree, its thick roots like elephants' trunks, and opened the seeds one by one. Bondeep sat on another root. They looked on, enchanted by the floating flecks of cottonwool. They did not think of the cremation ground nearby at all. The rhythm of new life touched their hearts. Not uttering a word, they left the place as the sun lazily dipped closer to the horizon.

That day when she returned home, she found Shontu-dada sitting in the front verandah. Without asking her a single question, he slapped her hard. There was silence all around her. She stood still in the courtyard like a piece of stone. Her mother witnessed it all. Now she dragged her inside and started scolding her. She accused Paridhi of becoming unmanageable day by day. Paridhi had made a great mistake by sitting with a young man in the lonely jungle. Shontu-dada at least stopped at slapping her. She should have been punished more. Her father was often accosted by people who remarked sarcastically, "Oh, your daughter has now grown up enough to ensnare young men."

Shontu-dada now joined her mother who was still furiously rebuking her. What did they talk about? Why did he take her to the simolu tree? He had to bow down in shame when people who saw them came to inform him. He was angry with his own father too. He had indulged her too much and spoiled her. If ever she was seen with him again, she was told she'd have her leg broken. Even the stationmaster was brought into the fray. He was a bachelor, could he be trusted? Why did he teach Paridhi to paint? What interest did he have? Why was he so fond of her? What were his intentions with her?

The words pierced Paridhi like thorns, but she did not shed a single tear. She sat, not uttering a word, mute as a stone. Did the world move around only with selfish interests? Did people have to have a nefarious purpose behind every action? Couldn't one person like another just like that?

In the evening, though it was warm, Paridhi covered herself with a sheet from head to toe while lying in the bed. She did not get up when her mother called her to have dinner. At night, her mother ran her fingers over her head tenderly. She turned her back to her.

"Tell me truthfully, did the boy touch you in a bad way?" her mother asked her anxiously, though her voice was soft.

Paridhi pretended to be asleep.

He didn't touch me with his hands but with his mind, Paridhi thought to herself.

Towards dawn, she had a dream. She saw her hands getting longer and longer. Then the hands reached the Simolu tree on the other side of the station and she hugged its broad trunk. The thorns pricked her, blood flowed down freely. But she still hugged the tree. Now a train stopped at the station. From its open windows she saw many hands waving at her. But she held onto the tree even harder.

She remained untamed by the people at home. That was an age when the heart ruled over the brain. It was also when her love for literature grew. The empathy brought the young boy and girl closer. They met from time to time at the station to converse. She almost wanted to tell him: "You touched me, and in my dream, I took a step."

The railway tracks listened to them, the open field listened to them. The sky above listened to them. The trees listened, the birds listened. The birds told the butterflies. The butterflies told the wildflowers. Perhaps their colour was spread by the wind all over the village. But they never uttered those three magic words, "I love you."

Their conversations were mostly about books, paintings and nature. Paridhi talked sadly about the dead little chicks of the Bortukula birds lying under the Simolu tree, she talked about a few wicked boys killing the monitors roaming around to eat their flesh. She lamented that the Teltupi birds were disappearing slowly.

At one time, in the cold Puh month when the sugarcanes flowered, at sunrise the flocks of little Teltupi descended on the field. Making a few rounds in the sky, they entered the sugarcane field and hung from the leaves. Their sweet smell pervaded the air. Every plant had at least fifteen to twenty birds. Greedy men brought long poles to thrash the trees and when the birds fell down, collected them in baskets to roast them later to eat.

He told her, "People aren't going to let anyone live. Those men are greedy enough to destroy lives. They are sometimes like fire, sometimes like the sound of huge waves. If people become like fire, you have to act like water; if they are like the howling sea, you have to be like the wind. The wind is not afraid of the howling sea."

Paridhi never tired of listening to him. One day she told him, "People don't take our sitting together and talking kindly."

"Oh, let them. It's easy to talk and pass negative comments. People can attack others—with their words, with their behaviour. They like to throw stones at others. Let them. Whether you'll build a wall with those stones, or a bridge, depends on you."

"Yes, it is your outlook, what you build out of the stones—a bridge or a wall."

Paridhi saw in the eyes of the college student a kind of determination. Her eyes were stuck on his fair feet, but she quickly averted them lest he caught her staring. When he talked, she stole looks at the faint green of his freshly shaved cheeks. Automatically her eyes slid down to his chest peeping through the shirt's open buttons. She became suddenly conscious of what she was doing and her throat constricted. Did he catch her inspecting him? The thought made her ears turn red in embarrassment.

He too sometimes looked at her with unblinking eyes while they talked. One day, when she waved her hand in front of his eyes to break the spell, he suddenly caught hold of her hand and looked deeply into her eyes.

"Oh! You shouldn't!" Paridhi protested, suddenly very shy now and freed her hands from him. Even after returning home, she could feel his hand holding hers.

This was the boy who completely took hold of her soul later. He also touched tenderly the body that personified her as Paridhi. They lost themselves in the magic of touch. Paridhi did not have any excuse to protest anymore.

Paridhi recalled now that young boy's face and its soft contours. She wanted to touch him again—that boy who told her one day that he liked her; that boy who expressed his desire to talk with her endlessly; that boy who looked at her spell-bound as they sat on the bench at the station platform, talking. He was the big shady tree that could ensure peace for her finally.

A light sleep slowly settled over her. The firefly was now gone. It must have found its way out.

16

"Your pebbles have now turned into butterflies. When are you coming to pick them up?"

"One of these days, promise! Lots of work piling up. Now tell me what you will cook for me."

"Well, since you don't eat meat or fish, let me think," Paridhi replied. After some time she wrote, "I'll cook yam leaves with small tomatoes, a dry curry of banana flower, Bok flowers and pumpkin flowers dipped in gram flour paste and fried till they're crispy, roasted brinjal with egg, lentil with curry leaves, chutney, and with it wulmukuta yam with mustard paste, bamboo-shoot pickle..."

"Okay, okay, enough!" Mayur laughed and did not let Paridhi continue with the list of items on her menu.

"You'll come for the day, right?"

"Yes, promise!"

"You guys make promises at the drop of a hat and then break them equally fast."

"I am not like that. I keep my word. Rather people don't

keep promises made to me. People hurt me." His voice seemed moist with sadness.

"Who? Who hasn't kept their word? Who hurt you?" Paridhi asked with real concern.

"Oh, let's leave it at that. I'll tell you one day. Bye now, we'll meet soon."

Mayur switched off the phone to stop her from asking further questions. As she ran the paintbrush over the wing of a butterfly to make it brighter, Paridhi wondered who had hurt Mayur. At times she felt that he wanted to tell her something but then held back. The boy who was in love with the wild seemed morose sometimes. Why? What troubled him? Otherwise he had a child-like smile always pasted on his face. When you saw his posts on Facebook, he looked as if he could light up the world with his smile. Even the butterflies in the forest fell in love with him perhaps.

Mayur had told her one day that at times he felt like living on the same plane as the butterflies. His profile photo on social media showed his face upturned towards the sky and a couple of butterflies resting on his cheeks. Seeing him like this, Paridhi felt as if he was not a human being but an angel and the butterflies were pretty dancers from heaven. When she told him this he laughed and said, "Whoa! What are you saying? I don't have the qualities of an angel. I am like any other person with hundreds of faults. But one thing I must say about myself, I haven't hurt anybody knowingly. I want everybody, whether humans, animals, birds, or insects even, to live happily. And as long as I live,

I'll try to make others happy, even in my sad moments."

Who could hurt a person like him, Paridhi wondered. If she asked him which one was his favourite butterfly, he changed the subject. Who had broken promises made to him?

Even Bondeep failed to keep his word these days. He seemed to forget the promises he made to her. The book fair was long over. He visited his house in the village at times and then returned to the city the same day. On his way he just stopped by Paridhi's house to have a cup of tea. Their plans to go somewhere for an outing was yet to materialise. Paridhi did not mention it. Often, she did not take his calls. Even when she did, she answered to his queries perfunctorily. Bondeep messaged her many times, "Why are you behaving like this? Why don't you tell me?" "Why are you offended?"

After many of these messages, Paridhi wrote: "Dreams, pain, life's struggles—all these are private. You can't make them less by sharing them with someone. You can only rest your head on somebody's shoulder, seeking solace, when an overwhelming tiredness takes over. But one shouldn't take it for granted that the shoulder will be offered forever. This is my life, this is my pain, this is my struggle. My dreams are also mine. Even the dead dreams are mine. The smell that emanates from these dead dreams is also mine to breathe alone."

Bondeep was taken by surprise at these frank words. It was not that he had never encountered Paridhi in this kind of a mood. Sure, he faced emotional barbs from her at times, but this was different.

"These days your messages are full of thorns," he wrote back in such instances.

"Do you give me an opportunity to bloom?" she replied.

Paridhi yearned to find the Bondeep he used to be. The boy who came back after four years and at every opportunity wanted to kiss her, draw her to his chest and talked of making her bloom with his love. He would talk to her over the phone for hours on end without wanting to stop. Sometimes he did not talk at all, but listened. Paridhi wondered if he had fallen asleep and would ask, "Ei! Are you awake? You are not saying anything at all."

"When the wind blows over the river one should only listen to the sound of the water."

Please get me back that boy again, Paridhi wanted to say. But whom to ask?

"Pari, somebody is ringing the calling bell. Please go, see."

She went outside and found the post-office peon dropping a letter on the chair. Picking it up, she recognised the fine handwriting of Station-khura.

The letter brightened her mood. He had written after a long time. After he got transferred from his post here, he wrote to her at intervals. He had now retired from service. He still lived alone. Once he had written: "Who is a better god than me? Without getting married I look after lots of children."

Station-khura taught a group of poor but eager children drawing and painting. He didn't charge anything for it, the children's joy was enough. He even bought the paper, paintbrushes and pencils himself. They called him 'Baba', father. That was satisfaction enough for him. Paridhi could well understand his happiness—a heart full of love does not need much money. In the letters, he hardly talked about himself but of the society, of people. He also updated her about the latest news on paintings. Paridhi had given him her phone number. But he did not call her, he did not divulge his phone number either, if at all he had one. He only wrote letters.

Paridhi opened the envelope and started reading:

> My dear Ma-joni! Please accept my love and blessings. I won't ask you how you are. All of us try to keep well in this life. But the way people quarrel and behave sometimes, it seems as if they are never going to die. People are getting sick and ugly fighting like this. They don't think of the land they live in, but hoard enough wealth to last for the future generations of their families. In a country where suicides by farmers make people bow down in sadness, its ministers move around in helicopters spending crores. And what about those leaders who shout from the rooftops promising to stand by poor farmers and labourers? They mouth a certain political philosophy but are blind to real-life problems. Then there are some writers who want to change society through their fiery writings but they themselves are corrupt. Everywhere you will see people changing their

colours. People are getting lazy, they don't do what they are supposed to do in their own field of work. The new generation is suffering from depression. Those who are well-to-do are sending their children away from the state. Most of them will probably never come back to work in their birthplace.

I see around here acres of land lying fallow. Young people don't want to take up farming. When I tell some of them that instead of leaving their own home, if they tried to bring modern technology to farming they could flourish, they look at me as if I am a mad man. But just think, is there anyone more independent than a farmer on his own land? Who keeps the land fertile? Who gives us sustenance? But they are regarded as much below in status compared to doctors and engineers. We give examples of countries abroad, but do we follow them? Over there a university reader's son works to earn his pocket money, a wife of a mechanical engineer works in somebody's house as a housekeeper. And here? Extra income only means bribes, *dadagiri*, middle-man, corruption.

Do you remember, one day you asked me why the borders in a man's atlas go on expanding? Why as an adult you don't find a map demarcated simply as in your childhood? Our geographical border is now embedded in terror and fear. At the hands of a few vengeful people humanity cries. But, isn't the colour of blood and sweat the same everywhere? As also of love and tears. And hunger too. People created religion for their own need. Then why do people kill each other in the name of religion? Why do people lose their way?

These things make me feel depressed, Ma-joni! Who will stay forever? What will they carry with them after death? The snake of death dances on a man's head all the time, man doesn't see it and so gets pleasure in acquisition and false hopes. Yet, there are good people, people who see the truth. Because of them, perhaps the world will survive. True, the battle between darkness and light will go on. At least in our hearts we should be able to carry on the light of hope.

I will stop now. Suddenly I felt like putting down my thoughts in words after a long time. I read your stories from time to time in magazines. I find both the subjects and language beautiful. Please continue writing. Continue talking about humanity and values. Oh, another thing. You'll be happy to know that my children are getting better at painting. After water colour, now they are learning to paint in acrylic and oil. I often tell them about you.

My love and blessings to you again,
Your
Station-khura

Paridhi finished reading the long letter in one breath, folded it and put it aside but the things he talked about stayed with her. Underneath people's artificial exterior, there lay fear, uncertainty. These negative forces trapped people in a sense of hopelessness. The newspapers and news channels made us believe that the air was poisoned with evil. There was no light anywhere.

But has society absolutely gone to the dogs? Have

people lost all goodness in their hearts? No, no, not all was hopeless. There were people who extended a hand of kindness and love to people in distress without any ulterior motive. People like Station-khura and Mayur, for example.

Paridhi had not seen Station-khura's adopted children, but they were familiar to her. Jupitora, Nazneen, Firhan, Dipu, Yasmeen and so many others. Imagining the children sitting with a canvas in front of them, intently mixing the colours, brightened her mood. Station-khura wanted to teach her oil painting but it did not happen. She didn't fare as well in the Matriculation exam and so people in the house were upset with her. Shontu-da was particularly angry. He blamed the paintings she was busy with, the books, her freedom to do as she wished. Indirectly, he also blamed the stationmaster and Bondeep. Her bordeuta did not admonish her. He only said, "I expected better results from you. But that's okay, try to do better next time."

Her father created a ruckus when she wanted to take admission in the Higher Secondary class. What was the use of studying further, he argued. She should rather learn household work and if a good match was found she should get married.

Paridhi was not surprised at all. She did not expect anything better from him anyway. When her uncle insisted that he would make sure she studied further, her father thumped his fist on the wooden bench he sat on forcefully and declared, "She is my daughter, it's my decision. Nobody else should interfere in this. Whether she studies further or gets married, I'll decide."

Like a madman he went on and on. Her uncle walked away from there. He was the one who had taken care of her school expenses. Paridhi managed to buy her painting paraphernalia and story books with her own money. She privately tutored a few young students. By then, she had learnt acrylic painting quite well. She painted designs on mekhela sadors and earned some money that way too. She filled her mother's boring white mekhela sador with flowers.

During that period, she painted a woman with acrylic paint on hand-made paper. Her black hair cascaded down her body like it was covered in many snakes . In her palm, she held an earthen lamp and the other palm covered it so that the light wouldn't get snuffed out. The soft yellow light of the lamp fell on her face.

Paridhi took a long time to bring about the effect of the light on the woman's face. The day Station-khura was leaving their place forever, Paridhi took along this painting as a parting gift. His eyes brimmed over as he took it from her hand. She could feel the unshed tears stinging her eyes. Station-khura held the painting delicately like he would a little child.

That day he left, she sat at the platform the whole afternoon. Juroni and Bondeep were also near her. But Paridhi felt detached from everyone. She was thinking of the man who had just left, a beautiful man with a beautiful mind. When she'd sat sadly because she got only a B Grade in the first year of her Higher Secondary exam, he had consoled her saying, "If someone can't get a good grade in the school of life, a plethora of degrees can't make him a real human being. So don't think that it's the end just because you didn't get the expected marks in the exam, and please don't think of jumping in the river to end your life like many others. Try to develop your own talent and lead life carrying the light within yourself."

Juroni was nudging her for some time, but her mind was elsewhere. Bondeep was asking her something, but she was too absorbed in thoughts about Station-Khura to hear him. He left the place in a huff. She followed him, asking "What did you say?" But he did not answer and walked on without looking back. He was offended. "Please wait," she shouted but he crossed to the other side of the railway track.

"What are you waiting for, you daughter of Baan? Go to your Aniruddha!" Juroni uttered dramatically as she pushed Paridhi towards the departing figure. Usha, daughter of the mythical King Baan of Tezpur, was in love with Aniruddha, Lord Krishna's grandson, and married him in secret.

It was as if Paridhi was waiting for her friend's encouragement. She ran; he looked back once but did not stop. He had now reached the corner under the Simolu tree. He leaned against the tree-trunk, one knee bent. After some time, Paridhi reached there too. She huffed and puffed and plonked down on one of the roots. When she looked at him, she found him watching the branches of the tree. Paridhi stood in front of him, held both her ears and asked,

"Shall I do sit-ups too? Am I being punished like a child in primary school?"

He stared at her kohl-lined, wide-open eyes for a long time and suddenly came close to cup her face in his palms. Paridhi did not have time to think. Then he had trapped her lips with his. Paridhi could feel a moistness spreading on her lips.

The sun was ready to depart for the day but paused a little. The breeze stopped blowing, the birds' chirping disappeared. Time stopped. There was only silence.

Back home, the sound of a great turmoil could be heard from the side of the road.

What had happened? Paridhi tried to guess. The sound became louder. From near the gate of Juroni's house, next to theirs, she could hear the sound of somebody running away. Paridhi was used to this kind of noise. People were always alert to these sounds, loud or more muted, coming from the side of the road. Even the sound of a tyre puncture made people run to their gates to see what was happening.

Paridhi had a vague idea that some people were on a protest march for something. She reached their gate. She could see a group of people in a procession coming her way. There were about twenty-five people in the group. Paridhi recognised them; they were from the village. They were shouting at the top of their voices. When she saw the person leading the procession, Paridhi did not take much time to guess the reason for the agitation.

Some time back, she had heard from someone that the platform of the railway station would be widened. For this, a Shiva temple which was at a little distance had to be demolished. Some people protested against it. Now they were conducting a *dharna* to submit their protest letter. They did not care for the comfort of the passengers. They wanted the Shiva temple to stay.

Paridhi craned her neck again. Now the procession was going towards the station, leaving the main road behind. She returned from the gate. Her uncle was sitting in the verandah. He asked her anxiously about the hullabaloo. She was reluctant but explained what was happening to him. The lines on his forehead gathered together. Paridhi knew a few moments later he would forget everything, a symptom that was escalating day by day. Sometimes he forgot her name even. He did not talk about his son and grandchildren much these days. Perhaps he was preparing to free himself from the attachments that relationships forge in a lifetime.

17

If life rains, I become a tree.
I write on my leaves
The story of water.
If life becomes a storm
I become a stone
I wrap within my heart
Stories of the ancient world.

"Wow! That's great! The jungle has turned you into a poet after all."

"Oh, come on, can you really call this a poem? I wrote it just like that one day, scribbled it on a piece of paper. Today I remembered it and wanted you to listen to it. I feel that the jungles themselves are poems. The trees, birds, flowers, vines, butterflies, grass, insects—all are verses in that poem. How can I do better than that? And also remember, the jungle will never abandon me."

Paridhi got up and ruffled his hair which was falling over his forehead. She said, "At last your promise to visit here has materialised."

"Were you waiting for me?"

"Yes, of course!"

"All these days I thought only the jungle waited for me," Mayur said and suddenly, as if he had remembered something, took out something from his jeans pocket and gave it to Paridhi.

A pebble. Paridhi felt its cool surface touch her outstretched palm. It was the size of borpitha, a pancake, grey in colour and smooth. A white line girdled it like an uttorio shawl.

"Brahmanshila," Mayur joked. Paridhi smiled.

Paridhi had seen this kind of stone, called Brahmanshila, in different sizes earlier too. A small one with three white lines was still lying somewhere in her purse. Then there was a big one, almost the size of a shaddock, where a thick white line ran through the middle. It looked as if the stone could be divided into two along that line.

"You seem to have thinned down," Mayur commented as he looked at her. She was wearing a long skirt in yellow, the colour of sonaru flowers, a cropped top crinkled at the neck and at the sleeves. Yes, she definitely looked thin.

"You also have black shadows under your eyes. Have you checked? Maybe the power of your glasses has increased?" he said.

It could be true. These days she did not sleep well at

night. She felt listless at times. Juroni's matter was another reason. Should she tell Mayur about her? Maybe then the heavy burden she carried inside her would become a little lighter? Nah, she abandoned the idea. Some sorrows cannot be shared.

"Wait! Are you going to examine me like this, or do you want to show me your manuscript?"

"Oh, sorry!" From his laptop bag he took out a spiral bound writing pad. Paridhi ran her eyes over it.

"Can you do something?" Mayur asked her.

"What? Tell me," Paridhi replied promptly.

"I was thinking I'd like to translate this book into Assamese so that children studying in vernacular medium schools could read it too. Can you do it? There's no hurry. Take your time."

"Okay, I'll do it. Who is he? I mean, the one who has written the Foreword."

She read the name at the bottom of the foreword again.

"Calvin. He is from South Africa. He teaches at the Johannesburg University. He has done a lot of work in the country for environment preservation. I often chat with him through email. Last year I met him at the 'Butterfly Convention'. He said Assam's natural beauty had enchanted him. He is such a simple, sensitive man!"

"Only the simple-hearted sensitive people can love nature truly. I at least think that nature-lovers cannot have ego or selfishness. Nature teaches man to be respectful and courteous. We feel how small we are when we are in nature's lap, its great power," Paridhi said.

"You are absolutely right," Mayur agreed. "I have met many environmentalists at home and abroad. The way they talk and behave absolutely captivates me. They do not show off their knowledge, they want to learn from others all the time, they say. You must have heard about the Butterfly Man, Isaac Kehimkar, long associated with the Bombay Natural History Society. A man simple and open hearted. He says going to the forest is his personal prayer. I also feel the same way. Before I enter the forest in search of the butterflies, I always join my hands in a prayer. Not to be safe from some impending danger but so that I am accepted by it. Whether we look for birds, animals or butterflies, we must become one with the surroundings. Sometimes we don't find anything we are looking for but continue hoping. The mystery of the forest pushes us to go forward. We are compelled to go."

"Do you know Mayur, you lead an enviable life," Paridhi said as she listened to him.

"Anybody can explore the jungle if they want, of course! You discover a new meaning of life. You know about Thoreau. He didn't go to the forest to live like the forest-dwellers; for him it was a place to develop his philosophy. Nature and man—they are both intrinsically intertwined. Modern technology-oriented lifestyle might try to distract people from this truth but to have a peaceful life there's no alternative to nature's company. She embraces without questioning those who feel lonely and loveless."

"And that's why you said one day, when the forest wind

touches the heart, you feel alive—it says, we are with you, don't worry," Paridhi recalled.

Mayur was about to say something but stopped abruptly, saying, "Let me take a picture." He walked towards the rongon flower bush. Paridhi too saw that there was a pretty butterfly resting on a flower. She went to have a closer look. The wings had patches in white and bright orange; a few black lines were etched on them and on the serrated edges in the triangles in black there were white threads.

"Leopard Lacewing," Mayur said softly.

"Aren't they flying jewels of nature?" Paridhi said.

"Yes. Isaac too calls them flying jewels."

Mayur smiled and turned the camera towards Paridhi now. She looked as if she was one of the flowers in the garden. He could not take his eyes off her. Paridhi did not notice. She ran her fingers softly on the blooms and asked casually, "Why don't you tell me who has hurt you?"

Mayur clicked the camera.

"You don't forget anything, do you?" he said. All of a sudden, he became very quiet. He went back to the verandah to sit on a chair. Paridhi too came back to sit next to him.

"The way you search for butterflies in the forest, I like to search in people's hearts. I like to bring up their stories from the unexplored depths of their hearts and help express them with my feelings," Paridhi thought to herself but did not articulate them in words.

"There was a butterfly I loved. I thought her colours

were mine too. We had planned to work together on many projects. But she went away. What could I do? I was helpless. Can you hold back someone who wants to go away? Or should one try to? But...even though time passes why can't the memories too pass into a forgotten land? If I could forget, I wouldn't have suffered like this. Her eyes were like yours—big, wide-open." Mayur shifted his eyes from the sky and looked at her.

Yes, her eyes were like that. She too loved the jungle. But did she sincerely? Mayur was not sure now. If one loved the openness of a jungle, could one give in to the temptation of a luxurious lifestyle? Yes, a life in the jungle is not all that romantic, it can be hard too. Those who want to work in the jungle must be ready for it. Even now, Mayur could not understand how a girl who wrote down on a pad 'Wanting less is a signature of richness' could tear off the threads of dreams they had knitted together and go away, looking for a sheltered life in the city.

Today he told Paridhi everything.

"We had planned to start libraries in the remote villages, provide free education to the poor children, start schemes of health insurance, and so on."

"She went away but she also left behind those dreams you had worked on together. How can you ignore those dreams? Don't they add meaning to life? Nobody knows when and whom one loses, whom you meet in life; nobody knows for whom one waits, or how life teaches love. But to live, we need those dreams, dreams that shadow us silently," Paridhi said.

Listening to her, Mayur told her about his dreams. He had so many things he wanted to do. Even the jungle won't allow him to die. But to fulfill some dreams you need money, you need commitment from others. He had been planning for some time to start a non-governmental organisation but for that he had to have projects. He was in talks with some seniors, they promised to help. He would teach students about the jungle. About GPS, GIS, Mapping, etc. Things that are necessary if you go into the jungle—how to enter the forest, what to do if you get lost, how to save yourself in case of possible dangers. Besides, the girls would have to be taught self-defense tactics too. At different places there would be centres to create awareness about butterflies—on their varieties as also the need for their preservation. He did not want anything for himself; he just wanted the next generation to love the jungle. If they learnt to love it, they themselves would come forward to preserve the forests.

"Anyway, I think like this—if we sincerely work at something good, even if we are not able to enjoy the sweet fruit of labour in our lifetime, the next generation will enjoy it. What else do we need?"

Paridhi listened to Mayur without interrupting him. She could not rest in peace either as she too had dreams of doing something beyond her humdrum life. She felt promise-bound to herself, to do something for the people. She wanted to share it with Mayur but decided not to. Instead, she said, "Let's have lunch now."

Mayur followed her like an obedient child.

"But be careful. Those who roam around the jungle are half-mad. They say whatever they want, and whenever," he said laughing.

In the afternoon, Paridhi accompanied Mayur to the railway station. On the way, they discussed the butterflies she had painted on the stones for him. He felt that she had shown a special skill in bringing out the various hues of the species called the 'Paris Peacock'.

He asked her why, if she loved painting so much, she did not pursue it more seriously.

What could she say?

"True, my dreams found their way into my paintbrush, but hard reality made me take up the pen."

She did not expand further on the topic.

Mayur did not push her. He looked around and followed her. For a long time, he had wanted to see the big Simolu tree. He had read about it in one of Paridhi's stories. The description touched his heart. When he told her about this, she promised to show the tree to him.

At the station, Paridhi stopped. The earth beneath her trembled as a blue train passed by. Like life's changing colours, the train's colour had also changed a long time ago. After the train left, they took to the path skirting the track. Paridhi looked towards the field in the distance and pointing, said, "Look, there's our big simolu tree!"

Mayur followed the direction she pointed in and looked at her puzzled. "Where?" he asked.

Paridhi was staring at the place with great intensity. Her eyes moistened. They did not see the small bushes at the border of the field. Through her tears, they looked like the grey watermark spreading on a paper wet with water.

"The tree isn't there anymore, but it is there," Paridhi said.

Mayur looked at her bewildered.

Can a tree's existence be so pervasive that even after its disappearance it can be felt? And the silence around announced its presence even now? The tree that stood there proudly for years and years, was not there anymore. The tree which had witnessed her days of happiness and sorrow was not there anymore. It was killed. Murdered. In the interest of man's greed that tree had been sacrificed. There was no one to protest or stand firm against this cruelty. The few who objected feebly were met with ridicule. The others stood, staring silently, the murder of a being that carried in its womb many diaries people wrote secretly.

Paridhi turned to Mayur and said, "You know, at times I feel a great emptiness. I can now show you only the base of the tree. A few days ago, a timber merchant bought the tree and chopped off the branches. A long time ago, however, there was talk of cutting this tree but..."

Paridhi stopped to catch her breath and then described

how the tree was associated with many legends, many incidents in the village.

She was then in class three. That day, there was a great hue and cry at dawn. There were police vans too. People whispered among themselves that Tilok-khura had burnt his wife, Swuoga-khuri, in the early morning. That Tilok-khura, who was the first one in the village to buy a television set, to whose house Paridhi had gone with her uncle to watch episodes of the *Mahabharata*. How could he burn his wife? Hearing the people talk about it, Paridhi felt her legs turn to jelly. The veins in her body jumped around and seemed to trap her body. She trembled uncontrollably.

Some memories are like stones that cannot be eroded even by the amnesia of time. It puzzled her no end how a simple, soft-spoken woman whom everybody loved could be burnt like this. How can a man do this to another person? Even today, the incident haunted her.

"We heard that after putting her on fire Tilok-khura tried to save her by covering her body with quilts and mattresses. But it was too late. Her body had turned into charred folds."

Paridhi was shocked that people went to have a look at that maimed body. The following day, feminist groups took out processions. Police, post-mortem, agitation, the cries of the 'killer khura', his own children's cries—all these unsettled the peaceful air of the village. All that remained of the woman's body was a skeleton. The burnt flesh had fallen off its frame. It was taken to the cremation ground near the simolu tree. The newspapers reported the incident next day. There was criticism from everywhere about the vile act.

It was said that for more than a month people heard somebody weeping around the cremation ground. The weeping turned into terrific screams that made the hair stand up on people's skins. In fear, the farmers finished their work at mid-day even though they had work in the field till the evening. It became a place to be avoided. One could hear dogs barking loudly from that side. At times, without rhyme or reason, a few branches of the simolu tree broke and fell down. All this terrified the villagers. The pet dog in Tilok khura's house started crying like a human being. Khuri was very fond of him. The howling did not stop for days. People could not bear it anymore and one day somebody poisoned the dog to stop it. It was buried near the place where Khuri was cremated. Because of this terrifying incident, the area around the simolu tree earned the reputation of being a place for ghosts. People avoided it. They believed that even if a body turned into ashes, its unhappy soul roamed in the nether world, and they took shelter in the old simolu tree. Whenever a body was cremated people seemed to hear sounds of laughter and crying coming out from the branches of the tree.

Even Paridhi was persecuted by the fear.

Another fear went round and round in her head. Nobody knew why Tilok khura had done it, but people said he lost his senses in a drunken stupor. She could not confide in anyone, but a fear cleaved through her heart. Suppose her father did the same to her mother?

"And then?" Mayur asked as Paridhi reminisced, now lost in her own head.

"Oh, after that? The family which owned the land where the tree stood thought of cutting down the tree. Everything was ready. But the woodcutters were scared of approaching the tree after hearing stories from the villagers. They were warned that it was a tree where unhappy spirits lived. They also would not be spared if they dared to cut it down. There was no tree cutting machine those days. Still scared, the poor labourers followed the owner's instruction to earn a few rupees. But as soon as two of them placed the hacksaw on the trunk they were thrown off as if by an unseen hand. They fell unconscious on the ground. The others ran away. That night, one of the labourers who tried to cut the tree had high fever and died the next day. The other vomitted blood after a few days and died. So nobody dared to cut down the tree after that. But ultimately..."

Without finishing the sentence Paridhi suddenly sat down on the track. "Why are we so helpless, Mayur?" she asked mournfully.

Paridhi was yet to accept that her simolu tree was not there anymore. Its disappearance had orphaned the village. She carried in her heart the emptiness of the place but could not express it. If she tried, the words disintegrated like the eggshells of the bortukola birds.

Under that tree, Paridhi had another experience that changed her life. How did she feel? It was as if something that had never happened, had happened to her. Everything around her seemed to stop moving. Once she woke up from that state, she pushed him away with a '*jah*!' and ran away. She could hear her heart thumping. It trembled with a feeling she could not explain to others.

After that she did not meet the boy. She even avoided going to the station. A shyness, an apprehension, took over. Juroni did not carry any news about him either. A plethora of questions and hurt feelings burdened her heart. Except for the time she spent with Juroni, she kept to herself immersed in her own thoughts. She meanwhile finished reading all the books in the library.

Paridhi's father had become less volatile by then. He looked sick and weak. He did not eat properly. But he could not quit his drinking habit. Her uncle tried to convince him to go to the doctor but the arrogant man refused. Unless absolutely necessary, Paridhi did not speak to him. Slowly, she noticed that he stopped being aggressive with her. Rather, when she stood in front of him, he could not meet her eyes. Did he suffer from a guilt complex because of Paras, Paridhi wondered sometimes. But no, one could not expect even that from this man.

One day her father told her mother, "My daughter doesn't acknowledge me as her father anymore."

"Whatever you say, he is your father, Pari! Why don't you talk to him? Don't be so cruel to him," her mother admonished her one day.

"Ma, just because he is my birth father doesn't mean he is my father in any real sense. My image of a father is of someone under whose care I can feel safe. From whom I can expect care, and not cruel words and a filthy smell," Paridhi replied without raising her voice.

After some days, as that same man tried to draw his last breath, he gestured to Paridhi to come near and indicated that he wanted to touch her head. Paridhi did as he wanted despite herself. He ran his fingers over her head. Tears streaked his cheeks. Those tears also softened her mind.

When she was in the second year in college, a marriage proposal came from a boy who was a distant relative of her bor-ma. Shontu-da and her aunt were very keen on the match. Nobody thought of asking for her consent. One day she grasped her bordeuta's feet and begged, "Please let me live, please let me live my way."

Her uncle understood the meaning behind her tears but Shontu-da did not bother. The groom-to-be was very rich. He liked Pari and would ensure that she lived a very comfortable life. Paridhi's simple mother also consented. The only comment she made was, "Hope he doesn't drink."

Her uncle was too gentle to make a hue and cry. Shontu-da did not bother to listen to him. Meanwhile preparations for the wedding went on. She often dreamt her old dream—of her hand reaching out to the simolu tree and hugging it. She also saw a face surfacing from underneath the tree. What should she do now? The freedom of the sky seemed to elude her; she was like a bird without wings. She seemed to walk on broken glass in a world where people did not accept others' wishes, others' aspirations. A great battle raged in her mind. On one hand, she was determined to be true to herself, on the other a woman's natural instinct to keep the people in the family happy even if it meant sacrificing her own self, drew her back.

But at last...

At last, she stood up gathering strength from within herself. She did not want to lose herself for the sake of a few unreasonable people. When the heart is reluctant, the colours that give sustenance to life also lose their purity. She was not ready to live with fake colours. She felt that if one kept the soul's door open nobody had the power or right to shut it with iron locks.

Paridhi somehow managed to obtain the address of the groom's house and wrote to them that she was unwilling to get married. The day people in her house came to know about this transgression, everybody, except her uncle, attacked her with words sharp as nails. She seemed to have committed an unforgivable sin. They stopped talking to her. Shontu-dada, in fact, even stopped her from going to college. In sadness and frustration, she wrote in her diary:

"People need people's company. But sometimes I feel like staying away from everyone I know and live cocooned in the company of books, pens, paints and music. But in the darkness, I also seek soft lullabies from my dear ones, I look for hands to console me. Sometimes I feel like the girl from the fable who went away to the hills to live on her own. We people on earth are different. But somewhere there is a similarity too. Perhaps it's the heart-wrenching feeling of not feeling safe among the very people who are your blood relations that rankles. This feeling of being abandoned silently eats into you and attacks your very existence."

During that period of loneliness Paridhi wrote her first story. Only now she fathomed the meaning of the words her Station-khura shared with her. She learnt to look for pearls in the deep sea of pain. And she learnt to appreciate life again. Her painting brush and the pen, both became intertwined in her desire to live.

The pearls were increasing in number. After reading her stories, some admirers wrote to her. Anuja-khuri too read her stories. She praised Paridhi. In those simple words of applause, she felt as if Anuja-khuri was standing next to her. Their exchange of letters continued. Anuja-khuri had opened a library in her own house, with her own money. She shared with Paridhi some of the great works she had kept in the library. Paridhi was happy that Anuja-khuri had at last shaped a life of her own. She never mentioned her husband, Prasanta. What was there to talk about anyway? He died suddenly in a bike accident. And Urvashi remained like that—in the same house—alone, her forehead bare of the red spot.

In the final year of her graduation, a letter arrived unexpectedly. A face came up from the folds of the letter.

It was a face Paridhi had carried with her secretly for the last four years with longing.

The face that she left behind four years ago underneath the simolu tree, wanting to see it again.

"After that day I never met you. You might think I have forgotten you. How can I? I love you, my dear. Do you still resent that without your consent that day I…"

Without finishing the letter Paridhi walked fast to the site of the simolu tree. There she felt as if all the colours inside her heart were crowding in, knocking urgently, wanting to come out. Then they emerged and climbed up and gathered on the branches of the tree. They transformed into red simolu flowers. They quickly bloomed to full glory and then dropped down. The seeds burst out and then…

Something precious she had thought she had lost now came back to her. Around her, the soft tufts of cottonwool were floating in the air. She shut her eyes.

Bondeep.

Bondeep.

Bondeep.

She pronounced the word again and again, savouring the sound of it.

That boy was Bondeep. The boy who told her a long time ago that he liked her; that he wanted to talk to her for a long, long time; the boy who sat at the station platform and spoke to her, staring deep into her eyes. That young boy who kissed her for the first time, standing under the Simolu tree. Who after four years ended her confusion by writing letter after letter. Whose love was like a hand that brought light to her heart.

"Look at this!"

Paridhi started as she heard Mayur's voice. The memory

of that day was still clinging to her eyes. She tried to be at ease and looked at the camera Mayur was holding up to frame her face. The blood red sun was hanging in the enchanted sky.

"When will your forehead wear this colour?" Mayur asked with his usual half-smile.

Paridhi did not say anything. She turned her face away. She did not know what to say. Sometimes she thought that once you enter family life love loses its pristine quality. The colours fade away slowly. Perhaps it is better to be free and just love.

Mayur was walking around, taking photographs.

"Peanuts, peanuts, peanuts," a vendor was shouting, a blue box that had a glass front hanging from his neck. From a house at a little distance that belonged to the cobbler, a few children came running out. They surrounded the peanut vendor. Mayur walked towards them. He took his purse out from the back pocket of his jeans and bought peanuts for them. Then he took a photograph of the children with the vendor.

Paridhi turned away from them. Her eyes caught sight of the red buckets full of sand hanging from an iron rod near the rest room of the station. It seemed to her that the buckets would soon dislodge from the iron rod and the sand would pour out, one grain at a time. Would the sand be able to extinguish the fire that burnt inside her, apprehensive that she could lose the person dearest to her? She had heard from others that Bondeep's mother was preparing to welcome Ananya as her daughter-in-law. A Brahmin girl. Both the families had been close for a long time. Bondeep himself had told her that Ananya liked him. At that time Paridhi had looked at him sternly and asked, "And, what about you?'

"Oh, how you do go on!" He tried to draw her towards him.

"You can't trust men," Paridhi spoke in fake anger. Disentangling herself from his embrace she continued, "If you tell me someday that you had spent a night with a prostitute, I could bear it. But if you tell me about loving somebody else, that'd be difficult to digest."

Though knowing fully well that the man was hers, could she bear the thought of sharing him with someone, even if only physically? Could she forsake those loving hands that spelled safety for her, for the satisfaction of the woman with a sandalwood paste spot on her forehead? Could she ever forget the sharp pain of the words that attacked her? She had felt like dying then.

One day, a letter Bondeep wrote to her fell into Shontu-dada's hand. He burst out in anger. Paridhi gulped down the poisonous words like a neelkontha. But the remarks made against Bondeep were difficult for her to bear. Shontu-dada said in no uncertain terms that Bondeep was playing with her emotions, he had other plans. He was a Brahmin in any case, and he was not going to marry her. He would discard her once he achieved his goal. She would be the victim and would be left with a bad reputation.

With time, Shontu-dada's resentment that she had rejected his choice of a groom for her had weakened somewhat, but on such occasions it resurfaced with a vengeance. He again accused her of rejecting a nice, rich groom. In front of her, he burnt Bondeep's letter. Paridhi lost her equilibrium and as she tried to catch hold of the letter, the fire singed her hand. For a long time, she ran her fingers over the ash on the ground. Her tears fell drop by drop over it. Even after that, Shontu-dada tormented her on many occasions for her association with Bondeep.

Now as she remembered these occasions, Paridhi felt like laughing. How meaningless were those threats! Their love was not such to give in to somebody's threats, their relationship was not as fragile as Shontu-dada had thought; it had a lot of weight.

Nobody can stop a river from running its course, can they? Like life, love is also like a phoenix, building itself anew.

"Let's go!" Mayur said as he put back the camera in his bag.

Paridhi emerged from her time warp and walked side by side with Mayur.

"By the time I reach home, it'll be quite late. Tomorrow morning I have to leave for Manipur," Mayur was saying as he picked up the laptop bag kept on the stone bench at the platform.

They passed the hog plum tree near the station and started walking on the long gravel road with patches missing from the surface. Mayur told her that he would go to Anini in the Dibang Valley next. Its magic silence often waved at him in his dreams. But the journey would be full of hardships.

When the soul yearns for something, it prods a man to go on. So he would surely go there, Paridhi thought, for it was a thirst that opened up the path of life.

18

Paridhi stopped abruptly as she entered the drawing room. Bondeep was sitting on the old wooden sofa and was turning the pages of a magazine.

"Why didn't you tell me you were coming?" Paridhi asked.

"Had I told you, you wouldn't have been caught... right?" Bondeep said looking at her.

"What are you talking about?"

"You are roaming around till late evening with your friend. Khuri did ask me to call you, but I didn't. I thought, why should I become a spoilsport guborua in the honeycomb."

"Oh, don't try to be sarcastic at the slightest opportunity."

"When I say something, my words are like thorns. But what about you? Your words are like delicate flowers?"

"It's a good idea. If you can think of thorns as flowers, it's a great feat."

"Oh, you look like a butterfly!" Bondeep commented as he looked at her from head to toe.

Paridhi understood why he compared her with a butterfly. She leaned on the handle of the sofa next to Bondeep and said, "Had I known you were coming I'd have asked Mayur to wait a little longer. He could have discussed his forthcoming book with you. He got a lift in a car while reaching our home and so he left. But it's okay; he will call you. Wait, let me bring the manuscript."

"Wait, we can talk about it later. There's something else we need to discuss. Please sit."

Bondeep looked sombre. He rubbed his cheeks agitatedly and said, "My mother is in talks with Ananya's parents without taking me into confidence. She has started emotionally blackmailing me too. It's a difficult situation at home for me. I don't feel like coming home these days."

Paridhi's mood changed instantly. She said quietly, "Why don't you explain to her patiently?"

"I've been doing that for many months now. But she refuses to listen. It's not easy to make her agree; you know her. Ridhi, I feel helpless. I don't want to lose you, and I don't want to lose my mother either. I don't know what to do."

"Deep, I can't fathom why a certain set of people don't understand that all these social customs are only meant to make man a good human being. If all our natural desires, our wishes, get squeezed by these rules and regulations where will the zest for living be? Can people live like this forever in sorrow, just for the sake of some age-old customs? Will people always be judged by who belongs to the upper caste and who to the lower?"

Bondeep wanted to say something but at that moment Paridhi's mother came in with cup of tea. She looked at Paridhi and said, "He said he won't take anything, just black tea with pepper powder."

"Why? Wait, let me fry some luchi."

"No, please don't. I don't feel like eating anything now."

Paridhi did not insist. In her mother's presence, Bondeep did not mention his mother again. "Has Bor-ta gone to sleep?" he asked casually.

"Yes. I'll have to feed him something after a while. You know Pari, he didn't recognise Bondeep when he went to meet him. He hasn't seen him for a long time."

She left the room.

"When did you draw this?" Bondeep asked as his eyes suddenly moved to the wall.

Paridhi looked at the painting. Two cherubs with big wings were sitting on the ground. They were looking upward at the sky and seemed to be deep in thought. Their skins were the colour of earth. In Paridhi's painting, the wings, resplendent with colour, were oversized compared to their small figures.

"Many years ago. This water colour was inspired by an oil painting of Raphael's. This was the painting Paras planned to use in a scene of his children's film," Paridhi said.

Hearing her, Bondeep straightened up in his seat; he became cautious. He knew that when Paras came up, Paridhi became emotional and her eyes would soon be brimming with tears. How could she stifle the pain of losing her brother twice? He came home but then she lost him forever.

Paras had returned after many years. He left by train one day without telling anyone and returned one day by train too. That day, the tears those at home shed were those of happiness. Paras looked very different now. At one time he was mad about cinema; now he himself looked like a cinema actor. Many people in the village rushed to Paridhi's house as the news of his arrival spread. They looked at him as if they had never seen him before. They listened to him with rapt attention as he described his adventures.

Paras said that at the time when he had disappeared, he felt as if someone was constantly waving at him to come away. He decided to free himself from the shackles that bound him to his life in the village and went to Guwahati. He took up jobs here and there, but he was restless. He saved some money and set off for Mumbai. Life was a struggle there too, but he survived. By chance he also appeared in brief shots as an 'extra' in a few Hindi films. He worked in a garage for survival.

One day he was reading aloud to another Assamese boy who worked with him, the dialogues of a script he had written himself. A man who had come to get his car serviced was standing nearby. He heard him and asked, "From which film is this dialogue?"

Paras was caught off-guard hearing someone addressing him in Assamese. He cleared his throat and said hesitantly, "It's not from a film. I have written it myself, articulating a few of my thoughts."

The man observed him keenly and then asked, "Your own thoughts? Do you write?"

"Not really. But I mentally compose screenplays for films all the time. I enjoy it."

The man then asked him about his family back home. He put Paras at ease. Without hesitation, Paras told him everything. The man listened quietly and then asked, "Are you willing to work with me?"

Paras was astonished at the offer. Now the person told Paras about himself. He was a filmmaker; he made small-budget art films. His works had received quite a few national awards. He lived in Mumbai with his family but visited his home in Assam often. He had also made a few documentaries on Assam.

The sensitive man must have sensed a spark in Paras. Perhaps destiny had ordained that he meet such a person, Paras thought. His life changed after that. He learnt a lot under the director's tutelage. One day, when Paras read out a script to the director, he was overwhelmed. His encouragement helped Paras emerge from his self-imposed boundaries. He also got to know the director's friends. They too encouraged him as they listened to his ideas. By then, he was quite a familiar figure in the cinema circuit. He could even take the responsibility of directing sometimes. He led a comfortable life now. His mentor was kind to him. For Paras, he became a father figure—a father he had sorely missed in his own life. He opened up a world for Paras that he had always aspired to secretly.

But the boy who left behind a life of frustration did not forget his land. He often remembered his mother, his sister and the village. Since he was comfortably off now, a sense of responsibility also worked in his mind. That's why he returned. His widowed mother as well as his sister breathed a sigh of relief.

Paras started work in Guwahati. At times he also went to Mumbai. When he was in the village, he took the lead in social work to improve the state of the place. He bought new books for the village library that had gone almost defunct and tried to get the children interested in reading. With his efforts, the local brewery was compelled to shut down.

He had many more plans for his village.

Then one day…

On his way home from Guwahati he went to the bazaar. It was his death knell. It took just a few seconds. A huge bomb at the Ganeshguri market, a busy hub, decimated everything. Amidst the pool of blood, pieces of raw flesh, and the burnt smell of bodies, the dominant colour was death…

People, with full lives and dreams, with voices that once spoke and sang and screamed, were just lifeless bodies now.

Perhaps time paused for a moment, trying to guess who they were before they met their end, what were their hopes, and their dreams.

Just one year. For only a year, the people in the house found their prodigal son back amongst them. In the name of the land's freedom the illogical, inhuman act committed by a few killed many. Among them was a young man who had dreamt of a better future for his village.

How could one bear this shearing pain? Like a forest fire, sorrow attacked Paridhi and her family. It burned bright and fast, engulfing their souls. Only they knew what kind of strength they needed to endure the pain and bring a semblance of normalcy back into their daily lives. They'd done it now for four years.

"These little boys look much thinner than Raphael's plump ones. But their wings here are much bigger than the ones the artist drew and much more colourful. The painting was lying somewhere. At places the colour had faded. I simply brought it out, repainted those patches and hung it here," Paridhi said, looking at it with wet eyes.

Paridhi had a secret dream built around this painting. She wanted to tell Bondeep but he was sitting with his elbow on the knees, his face between his palms, deep in thought. She decided against it. Time passed in silence.

Outside, the darkness was getting thicker. Paridhi looked at the courtyard and was about to get up and shut the door. Suddenly the Bhupen Hazarika ringtone came alive. She did not get up. Bondeep looked annoyed as he fished out the cellphone from his pocket and answered: "I am coming, Ma!"

Tick...tock...tick...tock...the old wall clock announced the relentless progression of time. Paridhi stayed rooted to the same place long after Bondeep had left. She felt too drained to move.

"I am coming, Ma!" Somehow the sentence whirled around her brain again and again.

What should she do now? What was the right thing to do? True, they both had been ready for a time like this. But now that the time had come and they had to make a decision, they were at a crossroads. Had he weakened in his resolution, the boy who was once ready to break down the walls of the fort? Had his resolute fist slackened? Were the iron rods that were once ready to strike the fort for her slipping away from him? Otherwise, why did he say, "Ridhi, I feel so helpless ...I don't know what I should do." Where was his conviction? Why didn't he say, "I am there for you, don't worry."

Were yesterday's feelings and beliefs true today too?

"Juroni is not very well, Pari. Her sister told me that they are thinking of bringing her home."

As her mother spoke, Paridhi woke up from her reverie. Worry lines quickly appeared on her already downcast face.

She forgot what she was thinking about a little while ago, about her troubles. She could only hear the words, "I want to live," over and over again, like a chant.

Paridhi felt overwhelmed by the great weight of sorrow. She could hear the endless *ghorr…ghorr…*sound of Juroni's sewing machine. The wheel that turned incessantly seemed tired at times, like it wanted to rest, but it went on, refusing to indulge in laziness.

For quite some time, Paridhi had noticed that Juroni looked rather pale. She seemed tired and not her usual bubbly self. In the evening, after returning from work, she took a light meal and retired to bed early. One day, when Paridhi visited her and complained that she had kept her waiting for a churidar set for too long, Juroni apologised saying she had a terrible back pain. Paridhi understood. Juroni stitched a suit overnight if Paridhi said it was urgent. So she must have really been suffering. These days, her visits to her house had dwindled. Paridhi herself went to meet her friend in her house. Juroni kept cutting material for stitching while talking to her.

A few days later, Juroni went away to her aunt's place in another town. Paridhi came to know the reason from her elder sister. There was a lesion on her breast which was not healing. There was someone who lived near her aunt's place who prescribed ayurvedic medicines for such ailments. Juroni wanted to consult him and stay there for a few days.

Days turned into weeks, then months.

One, two, then three months.

All the women in the village missed Juroni. She was an expert at turning out dresses that complemented their figures. If the customers took a few days to pay for the work, Juroni did not remind them. So they did not want to go to any other tailor.

Why was she gone for so long? Did it take so long to cure a wound? These days, Juroni was not active on Facebook either. Growing restless, Paridhi called her. She had tried to connect quite a few times earlier too. But the network connection in that place was weak; the voice broke often, and one could not hear properly.

"What's wrong with you?" Paridhi asked Juroni in an accusatory tone when the call finally when through.

"Nothing much, really. Don't worry, there's a boil. It will be cured soon."

"Where's the boil?"

"On my breast."

"On the breast? Where, tell me."

"On my left breast. It's not an abrasion, but a small lump. There's an opening at the top."

"Have you consulted a doctor?'

Juroni was silent.

"Tell me! Why aren't you telling me?" Paridhi scolded her impatiently.

"I showed him a long time ago."

"What did he say?'

"He asked me to go for an operation." Juroni paused for a moment and then continued, "It's too late, Pari! Lots of time has passed in between. Now whatever has to be done will be done here. Yesterday, the ayurved doctor squeezed out a lot of pus from the breast. He has given a medicinal cream to rub there every day."

Paridhi lost her temper. She knew something was seriously wrong and Juroni was still trusting traditional medicine, and letting the practitioner squeeze out pus from her breast! She was suffering so much but was not sharing it with anyone. For the last one and half years, Juroni had carried on with a cancerous growth and she didn't tell anyone.

"You've hidden it from me even? Me? So I was wrong in thinking that we could share everything! I am no one to you? I don't know Juroni, when the thread that has bound us together from childhood snapped." Paridhi's voice broke.

"Please Pari, don't say things like that. Promise! Nobody in this world can snap that thread. Besides you, who is there for me? For the people in the house I am just a tool to meet their needs. I never managed to find the wrestler to protect me. I've pondered a lot. I took time to consult a doctor too. I don't have much savings. I could borrow, yes, but if I don't survive? I couldn't burden my family with debt after my death. You know very well I spent a lot on things I liked—wore new dresses every day, enjoyed outings, enjoyed food I savoured. I don't have any more desires, Pari!"

Paridhi could not bring herself to say anything more. She could not respond to Juroni's voice. "Hello! Hello!"

After that call, she called Juroni a few times to force her to go to the doctor. Juroni avoided the topic altogether and talked about other things. So one day Paridhi visited her aunt's place, accompanying Juroni's elder sister. Even though she was sick, Juroni was not sitting around. She was busy with the sewing machine in her aunt's house too. Paridhi scolded her severely.

"I have to do it, you know!" was Juroni's only answer.

That day, Juroni led her to her room and shutting the door, took off her bra and showed her the lesion on her breast. A little above the nipple of the left breast, as Paridhi touched the reddish area, she shuddered. It was as if she had touched a piece of wood.

"It's so hard!" she exclaimed.

"It has solidified," Juroni said as if it was the most normal thing.

"Please go for the operation. Don't worry about the money, I'll arrange something. There are lots of people who don't just think about their own interests, Juroni. I know a few of them."

"I don't want to die owing money to anyone. And more importantly, the time for an operation is long over."

Paridhi could not control herself anymore. She cried her heart out. Her friend was made of a different metal, she smiled and wiped her tears. Before leaving, Paridhi wanted to give her a few thousand rupees from her savings that she had brought with her. Juroni hid her hands behind her back. She tried to stop her tears from flowing down her face. Juroni did not want to show her tears to anyone. She was wearing a crimson churidar set—the colour of a setting sun. That night, when she called Bondeep, Paridhi wept inconsolably. He spoke to her tenderly, long into the night.

She learnt a few days later that the pain in Juroni's body was getting unbearable. The pain had now spread to the left arm. She could not sleep at night due to the pain. She leaned back on the bedstead and spent the night in the same position.

The girl who laboured day and night was now too weak to be able to go even to the bathroom. The girl who worked incessantly like a buzzing bee was now confined to the bed, tossing from side to side. Her aunt's family took her to a hospital in Guwahati.

"What did the doctor say?" Paridhi already knew the answer but still asked.

"He has given medicine for a fortnight. He did some tests. He said only after the results come out will the treatment start. I know, Pari, there's no time either for treatment or to lie to oneself. But ... I still yearn to live, Pari. I really want to live," Juroni said haltingly.

Paridhi was not familiar with that tired voice.

Juroni was brought home.

Paridhi went to meet her, trembling inside. As she stepped into Juroni's room, an unpleasant smell greeted her. Where was that smell of the strong perfume Juroni wore all the time? Every time she visited her friend, a different scent used to assault her nostrils. Today in the unfamiliar whiff was mixed the signature of an untimely death. She took a few hesitant steps towards Juroni's bed. Her body was still, like in a morgue. Her hands and feet that once moved restlessly all the time were now motionless. The girl, who hated flies, did not have the energy now to shoo off the hovering flies with her breath. Her elder sister wiped her face with a wet cloth. Her breasts moved up and down fast. A few moments before Paridhi had arrived, the wounds on her breasts had burst open. From one of them, blood and pus had come out. Like the ruby seeds of a pomegranate, spots of blood stained the floor. Blood was still flowing from Juroni's breasts. Her sisters tried to change her kurta. The smell of raw blood surpassed the whiff of the aerosol.

Paridhi looked on mesmerised. How robust was the colour of blood, even brighter than the colour of the setting sun.

For the first time Paridhi realised colour could denote pain too. She was not sure whether she was trembling or the floor beneath her was shaking. It was not possible for her to stay in that room any longer. She did not even have the courage to look at the familiar faces in the room. She left, without saying goodbye to anyone.

After that day, Paridhi could not gather courage enough to step into that room.

A week later, lots of people gathered in the courtyard of Juroni's house. Many wept for her. Many touched her body for the last time, her face with the threaded eyebrows, a face that was treated to facials at regular intervals. A soft breast that had now turned into a hard stone. The wheels of the sewing machine had finally stopped moving.

A whiff of a luxurious perfume melted away into another world.

19

"The caterpillar dies so that the butterfly could be born. And, yet, the caterpillar lives in the butterfly and they are but one. So when I die, it will be that I have been transformed from the caterpillar of earth to the butterfly of the universe."

Mayur had sent the message on WhatsApp. American writer John Harricharan had written it.

Right then, a few colourful butterflies flitted across the sky in front of her. She looked at them, enchanted. Only a few days ago she had thought that all the butterflies in the world had disappeared, their wings perforated by cactus thorns. That they would never fly again.

It was afternoon.

Paridhi was sitting on her usual bench at the station's platform.

Many days had passed since she had stepped out of the house. She came out of her room now only when necessary. Darkness engulfed her. She felt utterly alone. Even her favourite pebbles could not bring her solace.

Paridhi wished that in these moments of utter sorrow, her own people would come to her to run their fingers on her head in compassion, hug her and assure her, "We are with you."

Two faces came up at these moments. One with a trembling hand running over her head to console her and another, a thin old woman in a white mekhela-sador who held her close to her chest. Anybody else…?

Bondeep?

From the darkness a face came up vaguely. Paridhi was surprised at herself. How could she push away the person without whom her life was meaningless, colourless? What prompted her to behave like that? The thought of not hurting Bondeep's mother? Or a determination not to be defeated? Was it her wounded pride in front of the person dearest to her heart?

She took her eyes off the sky and looked towards the field beyond. That huge tree that made one's blood quicken from top to toe at its very sight was not there anymore. The tree that gave birth to many fables, the tree people believed that the fiercest storm could not uproot, the tree under which she had sat and got lost in the mystery of nature, was not there. That tree that she dreamt of, was gone.

Thinking of that dream made her lips break into a sad smile.

She thought of the past few days. She had lost the will to live. The morose girl who had once sat at the platform waiting, was waiting once again. For the train. Once again, she wanted to go far, far away.

That day, Bondeep's mother suddenly appeared at their gate. Seeing her, Paridhi was struck dumb. She recovered quickly and politely asked her to come inside. Looking at her, Paridhi was not sure which way the wind was blowing.

The woman hesitated but came in and sat down. Then she said in a harsh voice, "I haven't come here to sit. I need to talk to you."

"Please tell me," Paridhi replied softly.

"Couldn't you find some other boy to love? My son was your only target? You know very well if he marries you he'll have to leave home. Otherwise our society will excommunicate me. I lost my husband at a young age. I have brought up my two sons with great difficulty. The elder son keeps away from the house. My younger son is my only..."

She paused a little and then, almost crying, said, "Please don't take him away from me. Please forget him. I am begging you, my dear!" she opened her palms as if asking for alms.

Until then, things were under control.

"Why are you saying like this?" Paridhi held her hands and said quietly, "Even if I forget him, your son won't be able to forget me, Ma! I don't think he'll be happy with anybody else. Don't you want your son to be happy? Do you want to see him suffering all through his life?"

The woman did not allow Paridhi to continue, she flared up. How did Paridhi dare to address her as 'Ma'?

She knew girls like her very well. Though they behaved like innocent girls on the surface, inwardly they planned how to entice men by showing off their bodies to good measure. She knew about their family too. Forget about caste, she was the daughter of a drunkard, a lecherous man. How could she welcome her as her daughter-in-law? She did not understand what Bondeep saw in her. She was not that good looking either. Only a girl like Ananya could match up to the handsome, fair Bondeep. She had gone to the astrologer to check the almanacs of both, it was a perfect match. Paridhi's family must know about some magic potion to trap men. If her son ever married her, she would hang herself.

The woman went on and on. A hot Sirocco wind from the desert seemed to engulf Paridhi. The words were like sharp spikes that pierced her heart. She wanted to shout: My father was a drunkard, true, but he was not a lecher. He never touched another woman. She wanted to counter many of the complaints but could not. Her voice disappeared.

How could she bring herself to counteract such narrowness?

The woman left eventually. Paridhi sat still. Only when a hand touched her shoulder, did she return to the present. Finding her mother standing behind her, she held onto her, hugging her tightly.

The days that followed were indescribably painful. In the past too, she had been attacked many times by life's cruelties. She had faced them then. But this time. the attack seemed almost lethal. She switched off everything—phone, Facebook, WhatsApp. Her life was meaningless, only full of losses. There was no safety net. She wanted to go to sleep and never wake up again. The hands that had previously brought stones to life now sought sleeping tablets.

Still.

Paridhi took her eyes off from the field beyond. Her eyes were glued to the railway track. Joydev had brought to an end his tortuous life on these tracks. His head and body lay separated between them.

People thought, at last his mother is free.

And his mother thought, he is free at last.

She stoically followed the death rituals of his mutilated body. His blood, no doubt mixed with alcohol, lay coagulated on the tracks till the next day.

Before her eyes now came up a scene: Two little girls jumping on the sleepers between the tracks. They were holding each other's hands and walking unsteadily. Suddenly one of them let go of the other's hand and put her ear on the track.

Now they were holding hands on the platform, waiting for the train to arrive. After a few moments the ground beneath them trembled. The train slowed down with a *ghot...ghot* sound. One of the girls let go of the friend's hand and ran to jump into a compartment. The other girl stood rooted to the ground. She knew people who leave on trains never returned.

Juroni wanted to open a boutique, Paridhi remembered.

"You'll see, one day even our chariali will have a boutique. You won't have to wait long," she had said one day. Paridhi looked then at the top she was wearing, patch-worked in three colours, joined skillfully with lace; a border of flowers ran down from the neck. It was unusual, unique. Juroni had such imagination, such skill. She had gifted Paridhi this top.

"You've gone too early, Juroni!" Paridhi said the words silently.

Another person Paridhi loved dearly was ready to leave on this train too. She took off her glasses and rubbed her eyes with her *dupatta*. Yesterday, her bordeuta had done something unthinkable. He had been telling her repeatedly to call his son to come to the village. She was unwilling, but to satisfy her uncle, she made her mother call Dipak from her phone. Nobody was sure why her uncle was so insistent that his son should come immediately. When they finally learnt the reason, it came as a surprise.

"Let this house remain as it is. Don't be unkind to Pari. Accept without argument her right to this house. One needs money to live, one needs a house. But people do not need a mountain of money, nor a palace. I am sure you won't face any problem if you don't get a share of this house."

Her uncle spoke the words with great difficulty and looked at his son as if he was begging. Perhaps Dipak did not have the heart to oppose his father's decision on his deathbed.

When he left, Paridhi sat near her uncle. "You didn't do the right thing, Bor-ta! You have denuded my position in front of Shontu-da. We two need only two rooms, we could have managed. You shouldn't have deprived your son," she said.

"Son!" her uncle pronounced the word with great disdain. Then he turned his back to her and faced the wall.

The rays of the sun were gold in autumn. The stone chips and heaps of sand piled near the station, to be used for widening the platform, shone in the light.

Paridhi looked at the sun. The same sun. The same colour. Yet it looked so different.

Today she felt free after a long time. The girl who seemed to drown in poisoned water had broken surface to breathe again. Like a conch-shell building a hard coating with its own secretions, she too could now build around herself a strong layer after fighting a battle with her tumultuous emotions.

Today, after a long time, she switched on her phone. Bondeep had been calling incessantly for many days. She had not responded. Messages came too. She did not reply. Perhaps he did not know of his mother's visit. Paridhi was not going to tell him either. She would never tell him the hurt his mother had caused her. She thought for a long time and picking up the phone started writing: "As a son you should have thought about the concerns of your mother, her wishes, her fears. I know, even if you don't tell me, that like me, you too are suffering from a dilemma. Your mother brought you up with great difficulty without the help of a husband. She expects a lot from you. You must pay your mother's debt. I don't want you to bring sorrow to her because of me. I too don't want to be guilty of causing her pain. I don't have to repeat what life gave me, what music I heard after you gave me love. My dreams found a place to flourish. Whenever I looked at the mirror and imagined a red spot between my eyebrows, a flight of red butterflies took off. But after some time, they started disappearing. In their place, sandalwood-coloured moths flew around in the room.

Even though when I think of leaving you I die within. I get divided in two. One adamant, the other philosophical, cynical. The first doesn't want to leave you. But the other gets ready for the sacrifice with eyes misted over. Is it easy to uproot a tree whose roots have gone so deep? I don't know how I will carry on without the shade of that tree. I don't know how I will survive being thrown out from my own orbit. Then I think, why not? Does love mean only to be next to each other? Does separation mean the end of love? I try to convince my adamant self which tries to cling on to you. I tell myself about that painting. The one I have been planning secretly to paint with the colour of your love. Perhaps my dream will find its central point in that painting. The colour you have bestowed on me is thick enough to last a lifetime without fading."

After writing the long message Paridhi read it again. What would Bondeep do now? No, no point thinking about it. If he could not break down the walls of the fort, could not tear off from his mother's emotional ties, she could not do anything about it. But she could not lose her way. She had to go on. She had to live. The lives she read about in her favourite books did not teach her to give up. Lots of people suffered more than her. She could not let them down. Time grinds stones to small particles. But do they disappear? No, they take another form, making them stronger, more enduring.

"The caterpillar dies so the butterfly can be born."

Paridhi repeated the words to herself and got up. She walked slowly towards the fishplate that joined the tracks. The railway track reminded her that life meant forward movement. You never knew how far it went, what lay ahead. But there certainly was something that lay there. The prospect of discovering the unknown excited you enough to go on.

Paridhi thought about the painting that slowly was taking shape in her mind. The red vermillion swastika that somebody drew on the wall of the old house was the base.

And the colours.

Paras had written the script of his children's film talking about those colours. His dream of making a film on the subject remained unfulfilled. Now she would give it shape in another way.

Mayur was right. To fulfill some dreams, you needed money. But people's goodwill could also help form the base of that dream. Paridhi believed in it sincerely.

She had to involve the memory of her bordeuta in that dream. His body was gone, but his memory lived on. She would have to repair the old house now ravaged by termites. The rooms were quite big, too big for two women actually. They did not need all of them.

As soon as she thought of this, she felt as if a the hands of children encircled her hugging her tight.

She would take them into her fold. She would lovingly colour the hidden wings on their backs nobody had seen. In the light of the colours, they would realise that they too belonged to the same sky, the same air, that the colour of their blood was the same as others'. She would light up the dark alleys of their lives as they walked forward.

The sun was on the verge of setting. Like children unwilling to head home after playing the whole day, its fading light hung on to the tufts of clouds in the sky. But a rebellious streak still escaped and touched her face. She was standing alone on the railway track.

END

Acknowledgements

A few people have contributed to making this journey a pleasurable experience. At first, I must thank Pranjal Kumar Mahanta of Aalibaat Publications, Guwahati, who reached out to me and sent Sarmistha Pritam's books, wondering if I could translate *Rang*, a well-received book in Assam which I had not yet read. I was hooked after reading the first chapter.

I appreciate Sarmistha's trust in me, insisting on my taking up the project. Her resilience and indomitable spirit, despite the physical challenges, to keep writing with hope and beauty also inspired me to take up the responsibility.

I was pleasantly surprised when Himanjali Sankar promptly responded after receiving the manuscript and showed interest in publishing it.

To Megha Mukherjee I owe a big thank you for her insightful editing.

I also thank Sneha Khaund, fellow translator, for her interest in my work in this field.

Last but not the least, I thank the readers for their continued support as I try to bring forth the flavour of the rich Assamese literature to a wider world.